THE WEIGHT OF GRACE

A NOVEL OF FAITH, REDEMPTION, AND GOD'S PROVISION

TIMOTHY K. FRANKLIN

STRONG HOPE
MEDIA

THE WEIGHT OF GRACE

Timothy K. Franklin

This is a work of fiction. Names, characters, places, and incidents either are the product of the author's imagination or are used fictitiously. Any resemblance to actual persons, living or dead, events, or locales is entirely coincidental.

First Edition: December 2025

ISBN: 979-8-9945378-0-0

*To my Mother, who blessed me with wisdom that illuminated my path
and encouragement that sustained my journey.
Everything I write begins with what you taught me.*

CHAPTER 1

SILENCE IN THE PARKING LOT

The parking lot of Riverside Manufacturing in Midfield, Pennsylvania, had never fallen silent at 7:00 a.m., but on that first Tuesday in March, two hundred men and women stood frozen in dread-filled stillness. Gravel crunched beneath their feet as they waited, caught between fear and uncertainty. Everyone sensed something terrible was about to unfold.

John Mitchell stood near the back of the crowd, his breath forming small puffs of clouds in the cold morning air, his hands shoved deep into the pockets of his work jacket. Around him, faces he'd known for fifteen years stared at the makeshift podium where management had gathered.

The usual morning banter about weekend plans and kids' soccer games had evaporated the moment they were called outside instead of clocking in.

"Thank you all for gathering," began Richard Hartnell, the CEO who had flown in from corporate headquarters in Pittsburgh. His suit probably cost more than John made in a month. "I'll be brief because I know you're all anxious to understand what's happening."

Anxious didn't begin to cover it.

"As of 8:00 a.m. this morning, Riverside Manufacturing will cease all operations. The company has filed for Chapter 7 bankruptcy, and effective immediately, all employees are terminated. You will receive a final payout by direct deposit on Friday, which will include all remaining wages and the compensation required under state and federal guidelines, along with information about COBRA and unemployment benefits."

The words landed like punches. Someone gasped. A woman sobbed. Dave Martinez, who had started the same week as John, turned and slammed his fist into the side of his truck. The metallic thud echoed across the lot.

"This can't be legal," someone shouted.

"I understand your anger," Hartnell continued, his voice maddeningly calm. "Human Resources will be available in the break room until noon today to answer any questions you may have and help you file the necessary paperwork. I'm truly sorry it's come to this."

John didn't hear the rest. The words had become white noise, a distant buzzing that couldn't penetrate the fog filling his mind.

Fifteen years.

He was twenty-three when he walked through those factory doors for the first time, nervous and eager, grateful for a job that paid well enough to support the family he and Jessie were planning. He worked his way up from the line to maintenance supervisor. He missed Emma's first steps because of a double shift and coached Caleb's T-ball team on Saturdays, even though Sunday was his only day off.

He had spent years learning new skills, taking on small projects, and even attending a vocational school to learn how to weld with precision and safety. He had learned all the necessary skills over time, gained practical experience on the job, and eventually he was promoted to maintenance supervisor, a role that required leadership, problem-solving, and a broad understanding of manufacturing equipment. He had made real sacrifices, spent many hours of his life at this place, and with no warning, they just ended it.

The crowd began to disperse. Some people headed inside to talk to HR while others stood in small clusters, trying to process what had just happened.

He shuffled through the lot, scattering gravel in all directions, but he hardly noticed. As he climbed into the cab of his truck, he sat there with his hands on the steering wheel and stared at the building that had been the center of his entire adult life.

He gripped the steering wheel, his hands turning white, his broad shoulders tense. At thirty-eight and just over six feet tall, he'd always had the solid build of a working man.

He caught his reflection in the rearview mirror. Hazel eyes, bloodshot and irritated, stared back at him. His jaw was clenched, temples graying. He barely recognized the face staring back.

Suddenly, his phone buzzed, pulling him away from his reflection. It was a text from Jessie, his wife: *How's your morning going? Love you!*

He stared at the words on the screen, imagining her on the other end. Blonde hair pulled back while she tackled her morning, those steady brown eyes focused and capable. She'd want the truth, but how could he put this into a text message? Better to tell her in person. He started the engine and pulled out of the parking lot without looking back.

The drive home took twenty minutes, but he barely registered the familiar route. His mind kept hitting a wall, unable to process what had just happened. *Unemployed.* The word felt foreign, like it belonged to someone else's life.

He drove past Midfield Elementary School, where Jessie worked part-time as a teacher's aide, the grocery store they shopped at every Saturday, and the church where they attended most Sundays, when he wasn't too tired. Everything looked the same, but nothing was ever going to be the same again.

Pulling into their driveway, he sat in the truck for a long time, staring at their small house. They'd bought it eight years ago, stretching their budget to make it work. Back then, the mortgage payment seemed manageable, but now it felt like a noose.

Through the kitchen window, he could see Jessie moving around, probably cleaning up from breakfast. She'd be surprised to see him home so early. Anticipating her reaction, he rehearsed the words in his head: The factory closed. I lost my job. We're going to be okay. But even in his mind, the last part sounded like a lie.

He climbed out of the truck and trudged to the front door, his legs heavy. The key turned in the lock with its familiar snick, and he stepped inside.

"John?" Jessie appeared in the kitchen doorway, dish towel in hand, her face brightening into a smile that immediately faltered when she saw his expression. "What's wrong? What happened?"

He opened his mouth to speak, but the words wouldn't come out. In three quick steps, she crossed the distance between them and took his hands in hers. Her fingers were warm and slightly damp from the dishes.

"Baby, you're scaring me. What is it?"

"The factory closed," his voice wavering between shock and anger. "They filed for bankruptcy and fired everyone."

Her eyes widened, and for a moment, she just stared at him. Then she pulled him into a tight hug, wrapping her arms around his waist. He stood there, his arms at his sides, unable to return the embrace. It felt like he was watching someone else's life fall apart, a tragedy unfolding in real time. And he was powerless to stop it or look away.

"Oh, John," she whispered against his chest. "I'm so sorry. But we'll figure this out. You'll find something else. You're good at what you do. Someone will hire you."

Jessie's optimism felt like sandpaper against his raw nerves, but he didn't say that. Instead, he gently extracted himself from her arms and walked to the kitchen table, sinking into one of the chairs. Jessie followed, sitting across from him, her hands reaching for his again.

"We should pray about this," she said, her voice gentle but certain. "God will provide. He always does."

He remained silent, his eyes fixed on their joined hands. Prayer. Right. When was the last time he'd actually prayed, really prayed, not just bowed his head while Jessie said grace? Weeks? Longer?

He started to pray, but the words felt clumsy in his mouth, like a language he'd once known but rarely spoke anymore. When had that happened?

He couldn't remember the last time he'd prayed alone, without her beside him, her voice carrying them both through the familiar rhythms.

"John," she said, squeezing his hands, "let's pray together before I go to work."

He nodded. She bowed her head, and John did the same, staring at the worn wood of their kitchen table. Her voice, when it came, was steady and full of a certainty he couldn't quite find in himself.

"Father God, we come to you in this moment of uncertainty and fear. We don't understand why this has happened, but we trust that you have a plan. Your Word says that you work all things together for good for those who love you, and we claim that promise right now. We ask that you would open doors for John, provide for our family, and give us peace in this storm. We trust you, Lord. We know you see us, and you haven't forgotten us. In Jesus' name, we pray. Amen."

"Amen," he echoed instinctively.

She looked up at him, her eyes shining with unshed tears and something else: hope, maybe, or certainty. "Your turn," she said softly.

His mind went blank. What was he supposed to say? Dear God, thanks for letting me lose my job. Thanks for putting my family at risk. Thanks for the fifteen years I gave to a company that threw me away like garbage. He swallowed hard.

"God, I... we need help. Please help us. Amen."

The prayer was superficial, and they both knew it. But she smiled anyway and squeezed his hands again. "He hears us, John. I know He does."

She glanced at the clock and stood. "I need to head to work. "She kissed his forehead. "It's going to be okay. We'll get through this." As she headed toward the door, John stared at the clock on the wall, still feeling as if this were all just a bad dream.

He heard the front door close, then her car start up and back down the driveway.

He wanted to believe her. He longed to feel the certainty that radiated from his wife like warmth from a fire. Instead, he felt cold and empty, like something essential had been carved out of him in that parking lot, hollowed out like a butcher preparing a cut of meat.

The house fell quiet after Jessie left, the kind of quiet that made every thought louder. John stood at the kitchen counter, going through the motions of making coffee, measuring the coffee, pouring water, pressing the button. The machine slowly came to life, gurgling and hissing, filling the silence with something that almost felt normal.

He carried his mug to the window above the sink, cradling it in both hands as he stared out at the backyard. The grass needed mowing. Weeds had grown up the fence, and it looked like the area had been abandoned to a jungle of growth, the back fence needed painting. Emma's bike lay on its side near the shed, right where she'd dropped it yesterday. Beyond the chain-link on his neighbors side he could see the rooflines of the neighborhood stretching out in familiar patterns.

How many of those families were in the same boat now? How many men were standing in their kitchens this morning, wondering the same thing he was?

He took a sip of coffee. It was too hot, burned his tongue a little, but he barely noticed.

What if he couldn't find another job? One that paid enough? The mortgage. The car payment. Groceries for four. Emma would need braces soon; the dentist had mentioned it at her last checkup. And Caleb's school supplies, Jessie's car insurance, the electric bill that seemed to climb higher every summer.

The list scrolled through his mind like credits at the end of a movie he didn't want to watch.

He set the mug down on the counter and gripped the edge of the sink. Outside, a dog barked. Someone's car door slammed. Life continued like nothing had changed, like the ground beneath everything hadn't just shifted.

But it had. And John had no idea what came next.

The afternoon passed in a blur of phone calls and paperwork. He filed for unemployment online, updated his resume, and started searching job boards. Every listing seemed to require either skills he didn't have or experience in industries he'd never even known existed. Manufacturing jobs were scarce, and the ones that were listed paid half what Riverside had.

At 3:30, the front door burst open, and Emma and Caleb tumbled in, backpacks bouncing, voices loud with the chaos of elementary school energy.

"Dad!" Caleb skidded to a stop in the kitchen doorway, seven years old and all elbows and knees, his unruly brown hair bouncing with the sudden halt. "You're home! Are you sick?"

"No, buddy, I'm not sick." John forced a smile. "Just had a short day at work."

He felt bad about telling a white lie about being home early, but what should he say? Sorry, buddy, but your dad just lost his job, along with his ability to pay the bills, put food on the table, and keep the lights on. So he had told the lie because he did not want to admit even to himself that his family might have a lot more to worry about soon.

A lie to spare his son from worry because kids often feel like even small problems are the end of the world. Caleb would find out soon enough; they all would. For now, for a little while longer, he could let his son believe everything was fine.

Emma, eleven and far too perceptive for her age, studied him with her mother's brown eyes. She had Jessie's blonde hair too, pulled into a ponytail, but her features were sharper, matching the quick intelligence that never missed a thing. "Is everything okay?"

"Everything's fine, sweetheart. How was school?"

"Fine." She didn't look convinced, but she let it drop, heading upstairs with her backpack.

Caleb, less concerned with adult subtleties, launched into a detailed account of the kickball game at recess. John listened with half his attention, making the appropriate sounds at the right times, while his mind raced through calculations: mortgage, utilities, groceries, car payment, insurance.

As the numbers piled up, it felt like walls closing in, and he couldn't see a way through them.

Jessie arrived home at 4:00, and they navigated the evening routine with forced normalcy. Dinner was spaghetti, Caleb's favorite, and the kids chattered about their day while he pushed pasta around his plate. Jessie stole glances at him, her expression a mixture of concern and something else: perhaps frustration or disappointment that he wasn't facing this challenge with more faith.

After they finished eating, they told Emma and Caleb about the factory closing down and Emma had a look on her face that suggested that she had known it all along. Caleb seemed to be unaware of John's earlier white lie; kids were resilient that way.

They finished the evening routine: dinner was cleared, the kids were bathed and tucked into bed, and Emma's worried question had been met with a reassuring lie. Now, John and Jessie sat at the kitchen table once again. The house was quiet except for the constant hum of the refrigerator and the occasional creak of old wood settling.

"We need to talk about this," She said, her hands wrapped around a mug of tea. "Really talk about it."

"What's there to talk about? I lost my job. I'll find another one. End of story."

"John," Jessie said, her voice patient but firm, "this isn't just about finding another job. This is about trusting God through it."

There it was. The thing he'd been avoiding all day. He rubbed his face with both hands. "Jess, I don't... I can't do the faith thing right now, okay? I need to focus on practical solutions."

"Faith is practical," she said, her voice had that slight hint of hurt. "God is our provider, not Riverside Manufacturing. He will take care of us."

"Will He?" The words came out sharper than he intended. "Because from where I'm sitting, it looks like He just let two hundred people lose their livelihoods. Where was He this morning when they told us the company was closing down?"

Jessie flinched, and he immediately regretted his tone. But he couldn't take it back, and part of him didn't want to. The anger felt better than the numbness.

"God doesn't cause bad things to happen," she said, her voice strained. "But He can use them for good. We just have to trust Him."

"You trust Him," John said, standing up. "I'm going to update my resume."

He left her sitting at the table and went down to the basement, where he'd set up a small office space. The computer hummed to life, and he looked at the blank document on the screen. John Mitchell. Fifteen years of experience in manufacturing. Skills: supervision, quality control, and maintenance. It all looked so inadequate, so easily replaceable.

He closed the document without saving it and opened a job search site instead. Two hours later, he'd applied to seventeen positions, most of which were long shots. His eyes burned from staring at the screen, and his head ached.

Upstairs, he could hear Jessie moving around, getting ready for bed. He should go up, apologize for snapping at her, hold her, and reassure her that they would get through this together. But he couldn't bring himself to move. The basement felt safer somehow, removed from the life upstairs that he was responsible for providing: food, shelter, clothing, and more than just the basics: security, stability, and hope for a future.

He leaned back in his chair and stared at the ceiling. Somewhere above him, Jessie was probably praying. She prayed every night, kneeling beside their bed as she had since they got married fifteen years ago. He used to find it endearing, the way she talked to God as if He were right there in the room with her. Now, it just made him feel inadequate, like he was failing at yet another thing he was supposed to be good at.

His voice barely rose above a whisper in the basement. "God... if you're up there, I could really use some help right now." The words seemed to hit the ceiling and bounce back, surrounding him like fallen leaves. Of course, there had to be someone listening? He'd spent years in church pews beside Jessie, mouthing prayers, but now he wondered if he'd just been playing along all this time because challenging her faith would have meant challenging everything else, and it was just easier to go along.

He waited, but there was no response, no sense of peace or presence, whatever it was that Jessie seemed to feel when she prayed. Just silence, the hum of the computer, and the weight of tomorrow pressing down on him.

He turned off the computer and climbed the stairs, moving quietly so he wouldn't wake anyone. In their bedroom, Jessie was already asleep, or pretending to be. He changed into his pajamas and slid into bed beside her, careful not to touch her. He lay on his back, staring at the ceiling in the darkness, wondering if God was listening.

If He was, He wasn't saying anything back.

The digital clock on the nightstand glowed 11:47 p.m. Then 12:03. Then 12:28. He watched the numbers change, his mind refusing to shut down, cycling through worst-case scenarios and impossible solutions. Beside him, Jessie's breathing was slow and even, peaceful in a way that John both envied and resented.

At 1:15 a.m., he gave up on sleep and went back downstairs. He made coffee he didn't need and sat at the kitchen table in the dark, his hands wrapped around the warm mug.

On the refrigerator, held up by a magnet shaped like a sunflower, was a drawing Emma had made in Sunday school last week. It depicted their family: four stick figures holding hands, standing in front of a house with a rainbow overhead. At the top, in Emma's careful printing: God keeps His promises.

He studied the drawing until his vision blurred. He wanted to believe it. He longed to feel the certainty that had allowed his daughter to draw that rainbow with such confidence. But all he felt was reality pressing in, cold and unforgiving, and the terrible suspicion that if God was keeping promises, He was keeping them for someone else.

The coffee grew cold in his hands. Outside, the March wind rattled the windows. In a few hours, the sun would rise. Mike Peterson would be out there with his lawnmower by eight, just like always. By nine, someone down the street would start up a leaf blower. The Saturday morning symphony of suburban normalcy would play on schedule, because that's what happens.

Life continues. The world keeps spinning. Day and night. Over and over again.

Nobody cared that John Mitchell had lost everything today. The Harrisons across the street didn't know. Mike Peterson didn't know. Even if they did, what difference would it make?

They'd offer sympathy, maybe, shake their heads, and say how terrible it was. Then they'd return to mowing their lawns and loading their kids into minivans, back to their safe, predictable, spinning lives, while his had come to a complete halt. Their lives were still running smoothly, still turning, moving along like clockwork. They'd execute their plans, mow the lawn on Saturday mornings, complain about traffic on the way to work, and argue over what to have for dinner. All the mundane, ordinary things that now seemed like a distant dream, luxuries he'd taken for granted. They had the comfort of routine, of knowing what tomorrow looked like. John didn't even know what the next day might bring.

He knew how the world worked. The bills wouldn't stop coming. The mortgage wouldn't pause out of compassion. Two hundred people had been discarded today like broken machinery, and the world had already moved on.

He clenched his fists, frustrated with himself. Since when had he given up before even trying? Since when had John Aron Mitchell allowed one catastrophic day to define him? Sitting here in the dark, defeated and hollow, he felt like less of a man than the one who had walked into that parking lot this morning. But what disturbed him more than his defeat was his reaction to Jessie's faith. She had been so certain, so confident that God would provide. And he had felt... nothing. Not comfort, not hope. Just emptiness.

When had that happened?

He'd gone to church almost every Sunday for as long as he could remember, stood beside Jessie during worship, and taught Caleb and Emma to pray before bed. But now, facing the first real crisis of his adult life, he realized he had nothing to draw on. No reserves of faith to carry him through. Had it always been this way? Had he simply been going through the motions all these years, attending services for Jessie, teaching prayers for the kids, but never truly believing any of it himself?

The thought was more unsettling than the layoff. At least losing his job was something done to him. This faithlessness, if that's what it was, had been his choice all along.

Another thought came to him without really meaning to think about it. Was he angry at God? Or was God angry at him? The question felt foolish the moment the thought had formed, then guilt rushed in behind it. He shouldn't be thinking this way. Staring at the ceiling in the darkened room, he willed himself to stop going in circles, and somewhere between the guilt and the exhaustion, sleep overtook him.

CHAPTER 2
UNANSWERED PRAYERS

Three weeks felt like an eternity since Riverside Manufacturing closed, and time dragged on painfully. Everything seemed to move at a snail's pace, and John felt like he was in a movie where the character moves slowly through each day, never actually accomplishing what he set out to do.

He had gone down to the employment office because, even though he had filed for benefits online, he still had to visit the office once a month. He had called it the unemployment office out of habit, and had been quickly reminded of its proper name by a clerk with a practiced smile, a crisp blazer, and a little brass nameplate that read *Margaret*.

The office smelled like a mixture of burnt coffee and desperation. He sat in a plastic chair that squeaked every time he shifted his weight, filling out forms that asked him to quantify his worth in boxes for education, experience, and references, as if any of it mattered when there were no jobs to apply for.

The first payment arrived on a Thursday; they had given him a card where benefits were electronically deposited. He would receive eleven weeks of small payments. Which served to remind him that every dollar spent had to be justified, carefully applied to a series of measurements. Do we really need this right now? Can we get this somewhere else at a lower price? The small payments might keep the lights on, maybe cover a few groceries. But the mortgage loomed like a storm on the horizon, and the car payment was already inching closer, impatient and unforgiving.

Each day felt like pushing a boulder uphill, knowing it would tumble back down the moment he stopped to rest.

What would he do if he stayed unemployed, still firing off hopeful applications into a void that never answered back? There had to be something, some hidden solution, some lifeline just beyond his line of sight. That was the hope he held onto, fragile but necessary: there had to be an answer, some way to keep the bills from swallowing him whole.

Forty-three applications. Forty-three carefully crafted cover letters explaining why he would be an asset to companies he'd never heard of, for jobs he wasn't entirely sure he understood. In return: twenty-seven automated rejections, fourteen silences that screamed louder than any "no," and two interviews that led nowhere. The latest rejection email dinged into his inbox with a sound effect that promised hope but delivered nothing.

"We appreciate your interest, but we've decided to move forward with other candidates whose qualifications more closely align with our needs." Translation: you're too old, too expensive, or too desperate. Maybe all three.

He closed the laptop harder than necessary and rubbed his eyes.

The basement had become his cave, his hiding place from the life unfolding upstairs. Down here, he didn't have to see Jessie's hopeful face every single morning, pretend everything was going to work out, or feel like a failure every time Emma asked if he'd found a job yet.

He knew better than to spend so much time in the shadows. The darkness had a way of making everything worse, his thoughts scattering like dust into the corners. Sometimes he imagined movement at the edge of his vision, shadows shifting, stretching, screeching and clawing like something out of a cheap horror movie. Yet he kept coming back anyway, sitting in it, breathing it in until he barely noticed it anymore. He was getting used to the darkness, and that should have frightened him.

"God, help me find work."

The words came out automatically, a reflex he'd developed over the past three weeks. Five words, repeated dozens of times a day, like a mantra or litany that brought no relief. At first, he'd tried longer prayers, the kind Jessie prayed, full of Scripture verses and faith declarations. But those had felt like lies in his mouth, so he'd whittled his prayers down to the bare minimum. Five words. A desperate telegram to a God who seemed to have changed His address without leaving a forwarding number.

He stood and stretched, his back protesting after too many hours hunched over the computer. Upstairs, the house was silent. Jessie would be asleep, her Bible resting on the nightstand where she'd left it after her evening devotions. She'd probably prayed for him tonight, like she did every night. The thought stirred a tangled mix of emotions: Gratitude and resentment mixed with shame.

"Enough of this," he whispered to himself as he climbed the stairs, moving quietly through the dark kitchen. Emma's drawing was still on the fridge, the rainbow mocking him with its cheerful words: "God keeps His promises." Did He? Because from where he stood, it looked like God had forgotten the Mitchell family even existed.

Morning came too early, announced by Caleb's thundering footsteps and the smell of coffee brewing. John had managed maybe two hours of sleep, and his head felt like it was stuffed with cotton. He dragged himself downstairs to find Jessie already dressed for work, her hair pulled back in a neat ponytail, moving through the kitchen with practiced efficiency.

"Morning," Jessie said, glancing at him with that look, the one that was trying to be encouraging but couldn't quite hide the worry. "Coffee's ready. Did you sleep at all?"

"Some." John poured himself a cup and leaned against the counter, watching Jessie pack the kids' lunches. "I'll pick them up from school today."

"You don't have to—" Jessie started.

"I want to," John interrupted quickly.

What he meant was: I need something to do, some way to feel useful, some reminder that I'm still their father, even if I can't provide for them.

Jessie nodded, understanding the subtext. She crossed to him and kissed his cheek, her hand resting briefly on his chest. "I'm praying for you. God's going to come through, John. I know He is."

John took a sip of coffee to avoid responding. What was he supposed to say? That her prayers felt like they were bouncing off the ceiling? That every "God's going to come through" felt like a reminder he wasn't good enough and yet another expectation he was failing to meet?

Emma appeared in the doorway, backpack already on, her face serious. "Dad? Can I ask you something?"

"Sure, sweetheart."

She hesitated for a moment, chewing her bottom lip, then asked, "Dad, is God mad at us?"

The question hit him like a fist to the gut. Jessie froze, lunch box in hand, her eyes wide.

"What?" John set down his coffee cup. "Why would you think that?"

"Because..." Emma's voice got smaller. "You lost your job, and you can't find a new one, and I heard you and Mom arguing the other night, and in Sunday school, Mrs. Patterson said that God takes care of His children, but it doesn't feel like He's taking care of us."

John opened his mouth, but no words came out. What should he say to her? That he'd been wondering the same thing? That he'd started to suspect God had better things to do than worry about the Mitchell family?

Jessie recovered first, setting down the lunch box and kneeling in front of Emma. "Oh, honey, no. God's not mad at us. He loves us so much. Sometimes things are hard, but that doesn't mean God isn't taking care of us. He's working, even when we can't see it."

"Then why won't He give Dad a job?" Emma's eyes were shining with tears. "I've been praying every night. Caleb, too. Why isn't God listening?"

John's heart lurched, and something slowly began to crack in the wall he had been building brick by brick. His daughter's faith, so pure and simple, was breaking against the rocks of reality. He wanted to tell her that God was listening, that everything would be okay, that her prayers mattered. But he was afraid the words would ring false, or worse, that his lack of faith might somehow be responsible for all their problems.

"God hears you, baby," Jessie said, pulling Emma into a hug. "He hears every prayer. His timing isn't always our timing, but He's faithful. He always keeps His promises."

Emma nodded against her mother's shoulder, but John could see the doubt in her eyes when she pulled back. She had heard these adult platitudes before. She was eleven years old, and that was enough to know when grown-ups were trying to make her feel better without answering the question.

"Come on," Jessie said, standing and smoothing Emma's hair. "You're going to be late for school. Where's your brother?"

"Bathroom," Emma said, her voice subdued but steadier now.

John watched them go, feeling as if he'd failed another crucial test. He should have been the one to reassure his daughter, to speak faith into her heart. But how could he give her something he wasn't sure he still had?

After Jessie left with the kids, the house fell into an oppressive silence. His phone buzzed with an unknown number, and his heart jumped. He answered on the second ring.

"Mr. Mitchell, this is Karen from Precision Manufacturing. We received your application for the maintenance supervisor position. Would you be available for an interview this afternoon at 2:00?"

His pulse quickened. "Yes, absolutely. I will be there."

"Excellent. Our facility is at 847 Industrial Park Drive. Ask for me at the front desk."

He hung up and stared at the phone. An interview, an actual interview, the first one in two weeks. Maybe this was it, maybe this was the answer to all those prayers.

He showered, shaved, and put on his interview clothes, the same navy suit he had worn to church for years. It still fit, barely. He'd grown thinner over the past few weeks, stress had carved it out of him. The suit now seemed to hang off him, revealing a too-skinny frame beneath the navy cloth.

The drive to Precision Manufacturing took thirty minutes. The facility was smaller than Riverside, older, with rust stains on the metal siding, but it was a job, it was hope.

Inside, the receptionist, Karen, smiled professionally. "Are you Mr. Mitchell?" John nodded. "Ok, great, have a seat. Mr. Brown will be with you shortly."

He sat in the waiting area, rehearsing answers to standard interview questions. What experience do you have? What are your strengths? Where do you see yourself in five years? The answers he went over in his mind felt wrong, but he had practiced them until they sounded almost convincing.

"Mr. Mitchell?" A man in his fifties appeared, extending his hand. "Tom Brown, thanks for coming in on short notice."

They shook hands, and John followed him down a narrow hallway to a small office cluttered with paperwork and coffee-stained mugs.

"So," Tom said, settling behind his desk, "tell me about your experience at Riverside."

John launched into his prepared speech about his fifteen years at the company, his progression from line worker to maintenance supervisor, and his skills in troubleshooting, team leadership, and quality control.

Tom nodded along, making notes, then he looked up. "And why are you looking to leave?"

"I am not looking to leave," John said carefully. "Riverside filed for Chapter 7 bankruptcy, and the entire facility closed."

"Ah." His expression shifted, something unreadable crossing his face. "I see, and how many other former Riverside employees are you competing with for other positions?"

The question caught him off guard. "I... I don't know, two hundred people were laid off."

"Right." Tom leaned back in his chair. "Here is the thing, Mr. Mitchell. You are the fourth Riverside guy I have interviewed this week. All of you have similar experiences, similar skills, and all of you are desperate for work."

The word stung: desperate.

"I am not desperate," John said, though they both knew it was not an honest answer. "I am qualified, I am experienced, I am..."

"You're overqualified," he interrupted, "for what we're paying. See, I need someone who will stick around, not someone who will jump ship the moment something better comes along, and let's be honest, you are not likely to stay here long term. You would take this job because you need it, but you would keep looking for something that pays what you used to make."

"That is not..."

"And there is another problem," He pulled out a sheet of paper. "I called your reference at Riverside." John felt like he was being sandbagged. What had been said? He didn't know, but from the look on his face, it was not all good. "He said some good things about you," continued Tom, "but I think what he did not say is a problem. I feel he liked you as a person, but he did not seem to have much to say about your work ethic."

The interview spiraled from there, and every answer John gave seemed wrong. Every qualification he mentioned was met with skepticism. By the time Tom Brown stood and extended his hand again, John knew it was over.

"We will be in touch," he said, the universal code for "do not call us," because we are not going to call you back.

John walked back to his truck in a daze. He sat in the parking lot, hands on the steering wheel, replaying every moment of the disaster.

Tom Brown must have known Riverside was closing, yet he still asked why John was leaving, as if he were completely unaware of the situation and needed an explanation. Then he said he had interviewed other Riverside guys for a job, and the entire thing just felt wrong. He also referred to his work ethic without even an ounce of proof or any specific example, which made it seem as though the whole conversation had been carefully staged to put him on the defensive.

He had heard stories about how sometimes the job interviewer used the interview process as a means of humiliating a prospect for a job, turning what should have been a fair evaluation into something cruel and unnecessary, an exercise in power, a deliberate test of how much discomfort a person could endure, a situation where another human being might be made to feel the full force of rejection and insignificance, as if they did not matter at all.

His phone buzzed. A text from Jessie: *How is it going? I am praying for you. I love you.*

He stared at the message. How was it going? He had just been told he was desperate, overqualified. He had been humiliated by a man who clearly enjoyed having power over someone who desperately needed a job.

He typed, "Fine. Love you too."

He drove home slowly, the hope he had felt that morning completely extinguished. If this was what interviews were going to be like, if this was how potential employers saw him, then he was in even more trouble than he had thought.

After the disaster of an interview, John stood in the kitchen, looking at Emma's drawing on the fridge as if it might hold some clue to his missing faith. "God keeps His promises." He stared at the artwork on the refrigerator, unable to look away from those hopeful colors.

"Where are You?" he whispered to the empty kitchen. "My daughter is scared. My wife is carrying all this alone. I'm drowning here. Where are You?"

The refrigerator hummed. The clock ticked. Outside, a car drove past. But from heaven, nothing. Just the same silence that had greeted his every prayer for the last three weeks.

He grabbed his laptop and returned to the job search, because what else was there to do?

By noon, he'd applied for six more positions, each form he filled out felt more futile than the last: Warehouse associate. Delivery driver. Retail manager. Jobs that would pay half what he'd made at Riverside, jobs he was overqualified for, jobs that would barely cover the mortgage. But beggars couldn't be choosers, and John Mitchell was definitely a beggar now.

His phone buzzed with another text from Jessie: *Don't forget to pick up the kids. Love you."*

He stared at the screen, then replied, *"Ok, will do. Love you too."*

At 3:15 p.m., he pulled into the elementary school's pickup lane. Cars idled in a long, slow-moving line, engines running. Parents waited with windows cracked, some scrolling through their phones, others chatting through open doors as the cool afternoon air drifted in. John eased forward a few feet at a time, watching for his kids among the clusters of students spilling onto the sidewalk.

John slumped in his seat, hoping no one would recognize him, ask how the job search was going, or offer that sympathetic head tilt and the inevitable "I'll pray for you."

He was so tired of people praying for him. If prayers worked, he'd have a job by now. If God were listening, something would have changed.

Emma and Caleb arrived, opening the door and climbing into the truck. He forced a smile. "Hey, guys. How was school?"

"Fine," Emma said with a flat voice. She'd been quieter since this morning, and John's heart ached. Everything he had built over the last fifteen years was just falling apart one white lie at a time.

Caleb, oblivious to the tension, launched into a story about science class and something involving vinegar and baking soda.

John listened with half his attention, making the appropriate sounds while his mind spun through the same tired calculations. One more week until the mortgage was due. Maybe he could convince the bank to give him an extension. After that, what? Moving the kids into some cramped apartment? Asking Jessie's parents for money? Admitting he'd failed as a provider, as a father, as a man?

All this worrying was not doing anyone any good. He concentrated on driving; that was better than worrying about all the things he had no control over.

Once home, the kids vanished to their rooms, backpacks and all. John found himself standing before the weathered yard shed. Inside waited his suburban arsenal: the push mower with its dull blade, a leaf blower, and all the other implements that helped maintain the illusion that everything was normal, that his life fit neatly into this neighborhood's expectations.

Dinner that night was tense. Jessie had made chicken and rice, and they sat around the table as they always did, but the usual laughter and ease were noticeably absent. Emma pushed food around her plate. Caleb talked about his day, filling the silence with seven-year-old enthusiasm. Jessie asked about his job search, and he gave vague, satisfactory answers that did not invite further conversation.

Later, after the kids were in bed, Jessie found John in the living room, staring at the TV without really watching it.

"We need to talk," she said, sitting beside him.

His stomach tightened. Those four words were probably responsible for every argument in human history, going all the way back to Eve and the quality of forbidden fruit. Nothing good ever started with "we need to talk."

"About what?" he said.

"About this." She gestured vaguely, encompassing everything: the house, their situation, the space that had grown between them. "About you pulling away from God when you need Him most."

"I'm not pulling away," John said, but even he could hear the uncertainty in his voice.

"John," Jessie said, her voice gentle but firm, "you've stopped praying with me. You barely spoke to anyone at church on Sunday. Emma asked if God was mad at us, and you couldn't even answer her."

"What was I supposed to say?" His voice began to rise despite his effort to stay calm. "That God's not mad, He's just ignoring us? That I've been praying for weeks, and nothing's changed? That maybe her Sunday school teacher is wrong, and God doesn't actually take care of His children?"

Jessie flinched. "You don't mean that."

"Don't I?" John stood, needing to move, to do something with the anger building inside him. He couldn't even have a normal conversation with his wife anymore, couldn't talk about all the problems that were eating him alive. "I've done everything right, Jess. I've applied to every job I can find. I've prayed. I've asked for help. And what's happened? Nothing. Absolutely nothing. So either God's not listening, He doesn't care, or I'm doing something wrong, and He's punishing me for it."

"God doesn't work like that," Jessie said, standing to face him. "He's not punishing you. This is just a hard season. But He's still faithful. His promises are still true."

"Are they?" John heard the bitterness in his voice and couldn't stop it. "Because I'm not seeing a lot of evidence of that. I'm seeing bills piling up, rejection emails, and hearing my daughter asking if God's mad at us. Where's the faithfulness in that?"

"Faith is about what you do not see," she said, her voice tight. "I know it is hard right now to trust Him but that is how God works."

"Well, it's not working very well right now," John said as he grabbed his jacket from the back of the couch. "I'm going for a drive."

"John, don't—"

He was already heading for the door. He had to get out, to escape the conversation, the house, the weight of Jessie's faith that felt like an accusation. He climbed into his truck and drove with no destination in mind, just away.

The streets were quiet at 9 p.m. on a Tuesday. He drove past the closed factory, its parking lot empty and dark. He drove past the church they attended most Sundays, its sign lit up with this week's sermon title: "Trusting God in the Storm." He drove past the elementary school, past the grocery store, past what used to be the familiar landmarks of his life.

Everything suddenly seemed foreign, as if he were driving through someone else's town, a place he no longer recognized. He ended up at the park where he used to take the kids when they were younger. The playground was silent, the swings hanging motionless in the cool March air. He parked and sat in the truck, staring at nothing.

"I don't understand," he said to the darkness. "I don't understand what You want from me. I'm trying. I'm doing everything I know how to do. Why won't You help me?"

The silence that answered felt heavier than usual, pressing

down on him, weighing on both mind and heart. He leaned his head against the steering wheel and felt something inside begin to give way. Not dramatically, not with tears or shouting, but slowly, quietly, like a lightbulb burning steadily until its last filament flickered out.

He'd been angry before. Frustrated. Scared. But this was different. This felt like the moment when hope began to change into something darker, when he started to wonder if maybe God had never been listening at all.

He hated himself for thinking it, for how he was treating his family, for the bitterness seeping into everything. He knew it was wrong, but he couldn't seem to stop the spiral. He couldn't pull out of this dive, no matter how hard he tried.

He sat in the truck for a long time, watching his breath fog up the windshield. When he finally drove home, it was past midnight. The house was dark except for the porch light Jessie had left on for him. Quietly letting himself in, he eased the door shut behind him. A dim light glowed from upstairs. He moved through the living room, avoiding the creaky floorboard near the stairs out of habit, and climbed up slowly, each step careful and silent.

The bedroom door was half open. Jessie lay asleep on top of the covers, still in her work clothes, her Bible open beside her on the bed. Her face looked peaceful in the soft glow of the bedside lamp she'd left on. Probably waiting up hours for him before exhaustion won.

He should go in, wake her gently, apologize for walking out, and tell her he was sorry for doubting. But he couldn't make himself do it. Couldn't face those eyes, even closed in sleep, knowing what he'd have to say when they opened.

Instead, he backed away from the doorway and headed back downstairs, past the kitchen, down to the basement. Where he belonged. Where he could avoid her eyes in the morning. Where cowards went.

The computer showed his email inbox. One new message. He felt a momentary jolt. Maybe this was it. Maybe this was the answer. But it was just another automated rejection. Thank you for your interest. We've decided to pursue other candidates.

"Thank you for your interest," he muttered, mocking the words on the screen. "We've decided to pursue other candidates."

He shoved back from the desk and spun in his chair, kicking off the floor to add momentum. The room blurred around him. Walls, ceiling, shadows all melting together in a dizzying spiral. About right, wasn't it? Disorienting. Out of control. Just like his life.

He kicked again, faster, until the basement became nothing but streaks of darkness and something else.

Movement. In the corner!

His feet slammed into the carpet, stopping the chair dead still. The room kept spinning, and for just a second, as his eyes struggled to focus, he thought he saw eyes staring back at him from the shadows.

He stood up fast. Too fast!

The dizziness struck like it had been lying in wait. His legs buckled, and he went down hard, hitting the floor with a grunt that knocked the air from his lungs.

He lay there for a moment, heart hammering, then snapped his head toward the corner, where he'd seen what? His eyes darted around the dark basement as he scrambled backward, hands sliding along the floor until his back hit the wall. Fumbling for the light switch, his fingers were clumsy with adrenaline.

A friend of his once had a raccoon that got into his basement when the back door was left open too long. Something furry brushed past him on the stairs in the dark. He felt a sharp pain near his ankle and he had fallen, broken his arm, and spent hours in the ER getting a cast and shots just in case of rabies. John had laughed about it at the time.

He wasn't laughing now.

The overhead light blazed on, flooding the basement with harsh fluorescence. He scanned every corner, every shadow behind the water heater and storage boxes.

Nothing. No raccoon. No open door. No furry intruder waiting to lunge.

But the uneasy feeling wouldn't leave. He had seen something, hadn't he? Not an animal. A blur. A shadow. Like smoke, but more solid. More intentional. Whatever it was had seemed purposeful, deliberate, not just a random shadow. For a fleeting instant, he could have sworn he'd glimpsed eyes watching him from the darkness.

He rubbed his hands against his eyes. Was he losing his mind? After all the stress, all the failures piling up, failing his family, failing to find work, failing in every way possible, was insanity next? Was this what a breakdown looked like?

He thought about Jessie somewhere above. She was sleeping, probably dreaming of answered prayers and God's faithfulness. Somewhere above, his children were sleeping, trusting that their father would be able to figure this out.

Down in the basement, John Mitchell sat alone, feeling the first real tendrils of despair wrap around his heart. He'd been treading water for weeks, but he could feel himself starting to sink. And God, if He was watching, wasn't throwing him a rope.

The clock on the wall ticked toward 1 a.m. Staring at the ceiling, John wondered how much longer he could keep pretending everything was going to be okay.

He was starting to suspect it wasn't.

The knowledge pressed down on him, a weight that seemed to grow heavier with each passing hour. What did a heart attack feel like, anyway? Was this it? The pressure, the tightness in his ribs, the sense that something vital was failing inside him?

He placed a hand over his heart and felt it beating too fast, too hard. Or maybe not hard enough. How would he even know the difference? Would it just stop? And if something really was wrong, could he wake Jessie in time? Or would she find him in the morning, cold on the basement floor?

The thought should have scared him. He should have been more concerned. Stress could kill, couldn't it? High blood pressure. Stroke. Heart attack. Wouldn't that be fitting? Dying of stress in the basement while applying to companies that didn't want him? The irony wasn't lost on him. Of all the ways he was failing his family, dying and leaving them with nothing felt like the cruelest one of all.

Instead, there was only a dull, gray acceptance. Maybe that would be easier. For everyone.

He closed his eyes and waited for his heart to decide what would happen next.

No. He shook his head, forcing the thought away.

This was absurd, dark thoughts in a dark space. He was physically fine, but how much longer could he keep hoping for a job offer, any job offer at all, when hope itself began to feel like a lie he told himself just to get through the night? John stared at the floor, the uncertainty pressing in on him.

He felt like a ghost wandering through a maze of unemployment and doubt, unsure which way to turn. He realized the path ahead was tangled with shadows of despair and began to wonder if there was a way through this mess or if this was a maze of dead ends with no real way out.

CHAPTER 3
THE MASK SLIPS

Sunday morning arrived with the insistent sound of church bells. A recording, no doubt, but playing the same hymns nonetheless. A hundred years ago, those would have been real bells, their iron voices ringing out across the countryside, calling the faithful. Families would have packed wagons with lunch baskets and Bibles, making their way over dirt roads to whitewashed churches. Now it was just speakers on a timer.

John thought about how quickly everything could change. One minute you have a good job earning good money, and the next you're out of a job, like those church bells that used to ring, now replaced with a digital player and a speaker.

He lay in bed, eyes open, staring at the ceiling.

Beside him, Jessie stirred awake. The clock read 7:43 a.m. Plenty of time to get ready for the 9:30 service. Plenty of time to put on the mask he'd been wearing for the past month.

"Morning," Jessie said softly. Her hand found his, fingers intertwining. "How'd you sleep?"

"Fine," he lied. He'd gotten maybe three hours, most of it fitful, his dreams a confused tangle of rejection emails and empty bank accounts.

She squeezed his hand. "We should get up. I want to make pancakes before church."

Church. The word hung in the air between them. He knew where this was headed. He'd been dreading it all week, ever since last Sunday when he'd sat through the service feeling like everyone was staring at him, wondering why God hadn't answered his prayers yet, judging his lack of faith.

"I'm not going," he said, the words out before he'd fully decided to say them.

She went still beside him. "What?"

"I'm not going to church today." He pulled his hand free and sat up, swinging his legs over the side of the bed. "I need to work on applications. There are a bunch of new postings I saw last night."

"John." Jessie sat up, her voice careful. "It's Sunday. You can work on applications later. We need to go to church as a family."

"You go. Take the kids. I'll stay here and be productive."

"Productive?" Her voice sharpened. "Or hiding from your faith?"

He stood, grabbing his jeans from the chair. "I'm not hiding. I'm being practical. We need money, not another sermon about trusting God."

"We need both," Jessie said, getting out of bed and crossing to him. "John, you can't just stop going to church because things are hard. That's when we need it most."

"Need what?" He pulled on his jeans, not looking at her. "Need to sit there and pretend everything's fine while people ask how the job search is going? Need to sing about God's faithfulness while our bank account empties? Need to listen to Pastor Mike tell us God has a plan when I can't see any evidence of one?"

"So that's it?" Her arms crossed over her chest. "You're just giving up? On church, on God, on—"

"I'm not giving up," he interrupted, finally meeting her eyes. "I'm just tired, Jess. I'm tired of pretending. I'm tired of praying prayers that don't get answered. I'm tired of feeling like a failure every time I walk through those church doors."

"Nobody thinks you're a failure."

He grabbed a T-shirt from the dresser, staring at it instead of her. "I don't feel comfortable there anymore. Every head that turns, every glance. I can feel them judging me. Measuring me. Thinking I've been weighed and found wanting."

"John, that's not what's happening. You're just—"

"Imagining it?" He pulled the shirt over his head. "Maybe. But I still don't need to spend two hours at church being reminded I'm not man enough to get the job done."

She was quiet for a moment, and when she spoke again, her voice was softer but no less firm. "The kids need to see you there. Emma especially. After what she asked the other day about God being mad at us? She needs to see that we're still showing up, still trusting, still—"

"Still lying to ourselves?" His voice rose. "Because that's what it feels like, Jess. It feels like we're all just pretending that God cares, that prayer works, that any of this matters."

"John Aron Mitchell." Her voice went hard in that unmistakable way when she became truly angry. "Don't you dare say that. Don't you dare let your fear and your pride slip into blasphemy."

"It's not blasphemy to tell the truth," he shot back. "It's not blasphemy to admit that I don't feel God anymore, that I don't know if He's listening, that I'm drowning and He's not—"

"He is listening!" Her voice rose, and he realized they were both shouting now, their words carrying through the thin walls to where the kids were probably waking up. "He's listening, John. Just because you can't see His plan doesn't mean He doesn't have one. Just because you're going through a hard time doesn't mean He's abandoned you."

"Then where is He?" John's voice cracked. "Where is He, Jess? Because I've been looking, and I can't find Him anywhere."

Jessie's eyes filled with tears, and he felt a stab of guilt. But he couldn't take it back, couldn't pretend he didn't mean it. The silence stretched between them, heavy with all the things they weren't saying.

Finally, she wiped her eyes and straightened her shoulders. "Fine. Stay home. But I'm taking the kids to church, and when they ask why Daddy isn't coming, I'm going to tell them you're not feeling well. Because I won't let your crisis of faith become theirs."

She walked past him to the bathroom and closed the door with a controlled click that was somehow worse than a slam. He stood in the middle of their bedroom, heart pounding, feeling like he'd just crossed some invisible line he couldn't come back from.

From down the hall, he heard Emma's door open. "Mom? Dad? Why are you yelling?"

He closed his eyes. Perfect. Just perfect.

He went to reassure Emma, but she'd slipped back into her room and shut the door. John moved just outside Jessies bathroom, he listened to the muffled sound of Jessie crying. "Jess?" he said softly.

Nothing.

He pressed his forehead against the door. Tried again. "Please, Jess."

Only silence answered him. He stood there for what felt like minutes, unsure what else to do. Then Emma's door opened. Footsteps and the creak of the stairs told him she and Caleb were heading down. He glanced once more at the closed bathroom door and headed down the stairs.

In the kitchen, they stood looking uncertain. Emma's eyes were red-rimmed; she'd been crying. Caleb clutched his stuffed dinosaur, something he only did when he was uncomfortable.

"Hey, guys," he said, forcing his voice to sound normal. "Who wants pancakes?"

"Are you and Mom fighting?" Emma asked, her voice small.

"No, sweetheart. We just disagreed. Adults do that sometimes. It's okay."

"It didn't sound okay," Emma said. "It sounded like you were really mad."

He knelt in front of her. "I'm not mad at Mom. I'm just going through a hard time right now, and sometimes that makes me say things I don't mean. But Mom and I are fine. We love each other, and we love you guys. Okay?"

Emma nodded, but she didn't look convinced. Caleb pressed closer to his sister, fingers twisting at the edge of his shirt.

Jessie came downstairs then, dressed for church in a blue dress he'd always liked. Her face was composed, but he saw the tightness around her eyes, the set of her jaw that meant she was holding herself together by force of will.

"Come on, kids," she said brightly. "Let's get some breakfast. We need to leave for church in an hour."

"Is Dad coming?" Caleb asked.

Jessie glanced at him, and he saw the challenge in her eyes. Tell them. Tell them you're choosing to stay home, to pull away, to give up.

"Dad's not feeling well," he heard himself say. "But you guys go and have fun in Sunday school, okay?"

It was a coward's answer, and John knew it. But Caleb nodded and climbed into his chair. Emma followed more slowly, her brown eyes fixed on John's face, intense and unblinking. He could feel the unspoken accusation in that stare: You made Mommy cry!

He looked away first, reaching for the orange juice in the refrigerator. This wasn't worth it. The tension, the hurt in Jessie's voice, Emma's disappointed gaze. Staying away from church wasn't worth any of it. He should have just gone, swallowed his pride. It was only two hours. Two hours of discomfort versus this mess he'd created.

But even knowing that, he couldn't seem to make himself say the words that would fix it.

They ate breakfast in near silence, the usual Sunday morning chaos replaced by a careful politeness that felt worse than the argument. He made pancakes and served them with a smile that felt like it might crack his face.

Jessie helped the kids get ready, her movements efficient and controlled. Nobody mentioned the elephant in the room.

At 9:15, Jessie herded the kids toward the door. Emma paused, turning back to him.

"Dad? Will you pray for us while we're at church?" The words struck him hard, like an arrow landing in his heart. He met his daughter's earnest gaze, saw the stubborn little flame of hope she still carried, and his resolve began to crack. "Of course, sweetheart," he said. The lie tasted like ash in his mouth. He felt as if he were not capable of getting it right; nothing felt normal anymore.

Emma smiled, small and fragile, and followed her mother out the door.

He watched through the window as they climbed into Jessie's car, as she backed out of the driveway without looking at the house, they drove away toward a God he wasn't sure he believed in anymore.

The house fell silent.

He stood in the empty kitchen, surrounded by the debris of breakfast, and felt the weight of his choices pressing down on him. He should have gone. He should have put on his mask and sat in that pew and pretended everything was fine for his kids, if not for himself. But he couldn't. He just couldn't.

He cleaned the kitchen mechanically, loading the dishwasher, wiping down the counters, doing anything to avoid thinking about what had just happened. But his mind wouldn't cooperate. It kept replaying the argument, Jessie's tears, Emma's question about prayer.

Will you pray for us while we're at church?

He looked at the clock. 9:35. They would be walking into the sanctuary now, finding their usual seats three rows from the back on the left side. Jessie would be smiling at people, accepting their greetings, deflecting questions about where John was with practiced ease. The kids would be heading to Sunday school, Emma to fifth grade, and Caleb to first.

And here he was, alone in his kitchen, having chosen isolation over community, doubt over faith, pride over humility.

"God," he said to the empty room, "if You're listening, I could really use some help here. Because I don't know what I'm doing anymore. I don't know how to keep going. I don't know how to believe when everything feels like it's falling apart."

The refrigerator hummed. The clock ticked. The furnace kicked on with a low rumble.

He waited. The house continued to hum and tick all around him, but heaven remained silent.

He grabbed his laptop and went to the basement because at least there he could pretend he was being productive.

By 11:00, he'd applied to three more jobs and refreshed his email approximately forty times. No responses. No interviews. No hope. Just the same grinding cycle of effort and rejection that had defined the past month of his life.

His phone buzzed. A text from Jessie: *Service is over. Taking kids for ice cream. Be home around 1:30.*

He stared at the message. Ice cream. A Sunday tradition they'd started when the kids were little: church, then ice cream at Scoops on Main Street. He'd missed it. He'd chosen to miss it.

He typed back: *Sounds good. See you then.*

Five words. Inadequate and distant. But what else was there to say?

He set the phone down and leaned back in his chair, staring at the ceiling. Above him, the house was silent and empty, a physical manifestation of the isolation he'd chosen. He had thought staying home would feel like relief, like freedom from the pressure of pretending. Instead, it felt like more failure to add to the growing list of things in his life that were out of control.

His phone buzzed again. This time it was a number he didn't recognize. His heart jumped, maybe a job, maybe an interview. But when he answered, it was a recorded message about an extended warranty. He hung up and tossed the phone onto the desk, where the paperwork and bills still waited.

"This is ridiculous," he muttered. "This is all ridiculous."

He stood and paced the small basement space, his mind racing. What was he doing? Sitting here alone, applying for jobs that wouldn't call back, avoiding his family, avoiding church, avoiding God. What was the point? What was any of this accomplishing except making him feel worse?

But going to church hadn't made him feel better either. Sitting in that pew, singing those songs, listening to sermons about faith and trust and God's provision, it had all felt like salt in an open wound. Every word was a reminder of what he didn't have, what he couldn't feel, what he was failing to believe.

His phone buzzed a third time. Another text from Jessie: *Emma wants to know if you're okay.*

He could picture it: Emma in the back seat of the car, ice cream cone in hand, worried about her father. Eleven years old and already carrying burdens she shouldn't have to carry. Because of him. Because he couldn't keep it together, couldn't maintain the façade, couldn't be the father and husband his family needed.

He typed: *Tell her I'm fine. Love you guys.*

Another lie. He wasn't fine. He was nowhere near fine. But what was he supposed to say? Tell her Daddy's having a crisis of faith and doesn't know if God exists anymore? That would go over well.

He set the phone down and returned to the computer, hunting more job listings with a forced determination he didn't really feel. If he couldn't have faith, at least he could have productivity. If he couldn't pray, at least he could apply. If he couldn't be spiritual, at least he could be practical.

The listings blurred together. Warehouse associate. Forklift operator. Shipping clerk. Retail manager. Customer service representative. Jobs that required experience he didn't have or paid wages that wouldn't cover their bills. But he applied anyway, filling out the same forms, writing the same cover letters, sending his resume into the void over and over again.

"God, help me find work."

The words came out automatically, and he almost laughed at the absurdity of it. He was sitting here, having just refused to go to church, having just told his wife he didn't feel God anymore, and he was still praying, still sending up that desperate five-word telegram to a God he wasn't sure was still listening.

Perhaps that was faith: the unwavering certainty Jessie carried, the innocent trust Emma bore. But this? This was something else altogether, a desperate, furious, doubt-ridden grasping at the faintest whisper of hope that someone, somewhere, might be listening.

Or maybe it was just habit, the muscle memory of a faith that slipped away so quietly he barely noticed until it was gone.

He remembered a story from Sunday school. The story of Samson and Delilah. A man undone by deception, his hair shorn away, and with it, his strength. Samson had marched into a fight with the Philistines, unaware that his strength had departed from him. It was a cautionary tale about what happens when faith is lost. However, there was more to the story of Samson and Delilah.

Something in the details that lingered on the edge of his mind, perhaps from a half-remembered sermon. There was more to the deception of Samson than just a woman who was faithful to the enemies of Samson. She had slowly badgered him, even harassed him, somehow convincing him that she would not betray him to those who sought to harm him. In the end, she had orchestrated his capture, and his eyes had been put out; he had been blinded.

Delilah did this for money, and the real reason why Samson was defeated and blinded was that he broke his vows. Samson, a Nazarite from birth, vowed to abstain from alcohol, dead things, and cutting his hair. He repeatedly broke those vows, allowing a woman to betray him by cutting his hair.

John pushed the thought away. Samson was a biblical narrative, a distant parable. His own losses felt more immediate, more brutal. A job. Possibly his marriage. The slow erosion of everything he'd believed in.

He didn't know anymore. He didn't know anything except that he was tired and scared and so far from the man he'd thought he was that he barely recognized himself.

At 1:30, he heard the car pull into the driveway. He climbed the stairs from the basement, emerging into the kitchen just as the front door opened. Caleb burst in first, his face sticky with chocolate ice cream, chattering about the story they'd heard in Sunday school.

"And then the walls just fell! Just from walking around and blowing trumpets! Isn't that cool, Dad?" Caleb marched around the kitchen in a solemn procession, chest out like a triumphant soldier of God.

"Very cool, buddy," he said, ruffling his son's hair.

Emma came in next, quieter, her eyes searching his face. "Are you feeling better?"

"Yeah, sweetheart. Much better."

The lie came easier this time, worn smooth by repetition. Too easy. When had he become so good at lying to his children? The thought made him sick. Not sick enough to tell the truth, apparently, but sick enough to recognize what he was becoming, a father who could look his eleven-year-old daughter in the eye and lie without hesitation. What kind of man took pride in that?

Jessie was last, carrying her Bible and purse, her face carefully neutral. She met his eyes for just a moment before looking away, and in that instant, he saw everything she wasn't saying: the hurt, the frustration, the fear that he was slipping away from her.

"How was church?" he asked, trying to sound normal.

"Good," she said, setting her things on the counter. "Pastor Mike preached on Job, about suffering and faith and trusting God even when we don't understand."

Of course he did. He felt a bitter laugh rise, but swallowed it down. "Sounds relevant."

"It was." She started unpacking the kids' Sunday school papers from her bag, dropping them onto the counter one by one. Each paper landed with what felt like a deliberate smack. "He talked about how Job never got answers to his questions."

The message was clear: she was angry, and she wasn't hiding it. He bit down on his response, forcing himself to stay quiet. Another fight was the last thing the kids needed to witness.

She continued, "But Job still worshiped. Still trusted. Still believed God was good even when his circumstances weren't."

He heard the message beneath the message. This is what you should be doing. This is what faith looks like. Why can't you be more like Job?

"Job kept trusting," Jessie said softly. "Even in the darkness. And God met him there."

"Well," John said, his voice tight, "Job got everything back at the end, his health, his wealth, his family. So I guess the moral is: suffer long enough, and God will eventually reward you?"

Jessie's eyes flashed. "That's not the point, and you know it."

"Do I?" He crossed his arms. "Because from where I'm standing, it looks like Job's story is about a man who lost everything, questioned God, and then got a cosmic lecture about how small and insignificant he was. And then, as a consolation prize, God gave him his stuff back. That's supposed to be encouraging?"

"John—"

"No, seriously. I want to understand. Because I've been doing everything right. I've been working hard, providing for my family, trying to be a good husband and father. And what happened? I lost my job. I can't find another one. My daughter thinks God is mad at us. My wife thinks I'm losing my faith. So what's the lesson here? What am I supposed to learn?"

Jessie glanced toward the living room, where the kids had gone to watch TV. She lowered her voice. "The lesson is that God is still God, even when life is hard. That His love isn't dependent on our circumstances. That faith means trusting Him even in the valley."

"Easy to say when you're not the one in the valley," he muttered.

"Excuse me?" Her voice quickly turned to ice. "You think I'm not in the valley, too? You think this is easy for me? Watching you pull away, watching our normal life disappear, worrying about how we're going to pay the mortgage, trying to keep the kids from being scared. You think I'm not suffering too?"

Shame washed over him. "Jess, I didn't mean—"

"But the difference is," she continued, her voice shaking now, "I'm not giving up. I'm not pulling away from God when I need Him most. I'm not refusing to go to church because it's uncomfortable. I'm fighting, John. I'm praying and believing and trusting even when it's hard. Even when I'm scared. Even when I don't understand."

"Good for you," he said, and immediately regretted it when he saw her face crumple.

"I can't do this," she whispered. "I can't carry both of us. I can't have enough faith for our whole family. I need you to fight too, John. I need you to at least try."

"I am trying," he said, but even he could hear how hollow and false it sounded.

Jessie shook her head, tears spilling over. "No, you're not. You're giving up. You're letting fear and pride and anger win. And I don't know how to help you if you won't even try."

She walked past him, heading upstairs, and he heard their bedroom door close with a soft click. He stood in the kitchen, alone again, feeling like he'd just failed another critical test he hadn't known he was taking.

From the living room came the sounds of the TV, some cartoon Caleb liked. Normal Sunday afternoon sounds. But nothing felt normal anymore. Everything felt fractured, broken, wrong.

He looked at the refrigerator, at Emma's drawing with its rainbow and its message. God keeps His promises. Did He? Because John had been promised that God would never leave him or forsake him. He'd been promised that God would provide for His children. He'd been promised that if he asked, it would be given to him.

But all he'd gotten was silence and rejection and a growing certainty that he was on his own.

He grabbed his jacket and keys.

"Emma, Caleb," he called toward the living room, "I'm going out for a bit. Be good for Mom."

"Where are you going?" Emma appeared in the doorway, her face worried.

"Just for a drive. I'll be back soon."

"But Dad—"

"I'll be back soon," he repeated and walked out before she could ask anything else.

He drove without a destination, his hands tight on the steering wheel. Past the closed factory. Past the church, where a few cars still lingered in the parking lot, people were chatting after service, living their normal lives with their intact faith. Past the elementary school. Past the park.

Everything looked the same as it had a month ago, but he felt like he was seeing it through a stranger's eyes. This town, this life, this faith, it all felt foreign now, like a costume he'd been wearing that no longer fit.

He ended up in the church parking lot, though he hadn't consciously decided to go there. The building sat quiet and empty now, its white siding bright in the afternoon sun. He stared at it through his windshield, this place where he'd been baptized at sixteen, where he'd married Jessie, where his kids had been dedicated as babies.

It should mean something. It should feel like home, like a sanctuary, like a place where he belonged. Instead, it just looked like a building. Four walls and a roof and a cross on top. Nothing special. Nothing sacred. Just a place where people gathered to sing songs and tell themselves that God cared about their problems.

His phone buzzed. A text from Jessie: *Where are you?*

He stared at the message, his thumb hovering over the keyboard. Where was he? Physically, he was in the church parking lot. Spiritually, he was somewhere much darker, much farther away.

He typed: Just driving. Need to clear my head. Be home soon.

Another lie. Another evasion. Another brick in the wall he was building between himself and everyone who loved him.

He set the phone down and leaned his head back against the seat, closing his eyes. He was so tired. Tired of pretending, tired of failing, tired of feeling like he was drowning while everyone around him kept telling him to just swim harder, just have more faith, just trust God more.

"I don't know how," he whispered to the empty truck. "I don't know how to trust You when You feel so far away. I don't know how to have faith when nothing makes sense. I don't know how to keep going when every door keeps slamming in my face."

Only silence answered, or maybe it was just the kind of silence that happened when you didnt' put in the right kind of effort. Maybe there was no one listening at all, maybe he was just talking to himself, hoping for an echo that would never come.

He opened his eyes and looked at the church one more time.

Then he started the engine and drove away, leaving it behind like he was leaving everything else: his faith, his hope, his certainty that God was good and life made sense and everything would work out in the end.

He drove home slowly, dreading what waited for him when he got home, the hurt in Jessie's eyes, the worry in Emma's face, the weight of being a husband and father when he felt like he was barely holding himself together.

When he pulled into the driveway, he sat in the truck for a long while, gathering the strength to go inside. Through the window, he could see Jessie in the kitchen, probably starting dinner. Normal Sunday routine. Normal life.

The problem was normal life had ceased to exist for John Mitchell.

He climbed out of the truck and walked to the door, each step heavier than the last. Inside, he could hear the TV and the kids laughing at something. He could smell dinner cooking, chicken, maybe. All the trappings of what used to be typical Sunday evening.

But as he stepped through the door, he felt like a stranger entering someone else's life. A fraud. A failure. A man who'd lost his job and his faith, his way, all in the space of a few weeks.

And the worst part was, he didn't know how to find his way back.

CHAPTER 4
THE DARKNESS OF PRIDE

The pizza box was warm against John's hands as he climbed the front steps of a two-story colonial on Maple Street. Through the window, he could see a family gathered around a dining room table: Mom, Dad, two kids, all of them laughing at something. A normal Tuesday night, the kind of night he used to have before his life fell apart.

He rang the doorbell and waited, adjusting his red DeliverEats cap. It had been six weeks since Riverside closed, six weeks of rejection emails, dwindling savings, and desperate measures. That was how John Mitchell, a former maintenance supervisor with fifteen years of experience, had ended up delivering pizza at 7:30 on a Tuesday night.

The door opened, and a man about John's age appeared. He was wearing a button-down shirt and khakis, probably just home from work. A real job, the kind with benefits, a salary and a future.

"Pizza delivery," he said, forcing his voice to sound normal as he held out the box.

The man reached for it, and as their eyes met, his expression shifted with a flicker of recognition, then confusion. John felt his stomach drop. Recognition. Please, God, not recognition.

"John? John Mitchell?"

His jaw tightened. "Hey, Dave."

Dave Johnson. They'd been in the same Sunday school class growing up and had played on the same Little League team. Dave had gone to college, gotten a degree in business, and now worked at some tech company in Harrisburg. And here was John Mitchell, delivering his dinner.

"Man, I heard about Riverside," Dave said, his voice dropping into that sympathetic tone John had learned to hate, "that's rough. How's the job search going?"

"Fine," he lied, shifting the pizza box slightly, "just doing this on the side for extra cash."

It wasn't technically a lie. He was doing other things too: handyman jobs through TaskRabbit, yard work, anything that paid, but extra cash implied he had a main source of income, which he didn't.

"Well, good for you, man. Staying busy is the key." Dave took the pizza, still holding the door open. "Hey, we should grab coffee sometime and catch up."

"Yeah, definitely," he said, knowing they never would.

"Enjoy your pizza," Dave said as he quickly turned and walked back to his truck before Dave could say anything else, before the pity in his eyes could burn any deeper. He climbed into the cab of his truck and sat there for a moment, his hands gripping the steering wheel as he tried to breathe through the humiliation.

Good for you, staying busy. Like he was choosing this, like delivering pizza was some kind of entrepreneurial side hustle instead of what it actually was: desperation, the gig economy's way of saying, "We'll let you work, but we won't give you dignity."

He watched in the side mirror as Dave jogged back out, wallet in hand. John wanted to disappear, to just be invisible, but he knew that look, the one that came before the gesture, the generous tip offered like a lifeline to a drowning man. His hands tightened on the steering wheel as pride and need began to fight inside his mind, but he already knew which would win.

He couldn't take it and wouldn't take it, not from Dave, not when it would confirm what the pity in his eyes already suggested: that John was someone to be pitied or helped. John rolled down the window as Dave got closer. "I always give a tip," Dave said, holding out a ten-dollar bill. "It's not much, but I was serious about having coffee.

You still have my phone number, right?" John took the money, the easier choice. Ten dollars wasn't charity disguised as a tip; it was just a tip, small and ordinary. John managed a smile. "Yeah, I still have it. Thanks, Dave, " he said, folding the bill into his jacket pocket. "Seriously, though, let's meet for coffee soon," Dave said. "Next week, maybe? Just give me a call."

"Yeah, I will," John said, even though he knew he wouldn't.

Dave nodded and headed back up the driveway.

John rolled up the window and sat there for a moment. His phone buzzed with the next delivery, another address, another pizza, another chance to run into someone from his old life. He started the engine and pulled away from the colonial, with its happy family and its normal Tuesday night.

By 10:00 p.m., he had made eight more deliveries and earned $47 in tips. Minus gas and the wear on his truck, he would probably net about thirty bucks. Three hours of work for thirty dollars.

The math was impossible, and he knew it, but what choice did he have? The unemployment checks helped, but they weren't enough, not even close. So he drove for DeliverEats in the evenings, did handyman jobs on weekends, and spent his days applying for real jobs that never called back.

At this rate, he would need to work ninety hours a week just to cover the mortgage.

He pulled into his driveway at 10:23, exhausted and smelling like pepperoni. Through the living room window, he could see Jessie on the couch, her laptop open, probably grading papers. She had been working more hours at the school, picking up extra duties and doing whatever she could to help keep them afloat.

He sat in the truck for a moment, not ready to go inside, not ready to see the question in Jessie's eyes: How much did you make tonight? Is it enough? The answer was always no. It wasn't enough. It would never be enough. His phone buzzed with a text from Jessie: *I can see you sitting in the truck. Come inside.*

He sighed and climbed out, grabbing his DeliverEats bag from the passenger seat. Inside, the house was quiet, and the kids were asleep. Jessie looked up from her laptop as he entered, her face tired but trying to smile.

"How'd it go?" she asked.

"Fine, made some tips." He pulled a crumpled wad of bills from his pocket and set them on the coffee table: three tens, two fives, and a handful of ones, forty-seven dollars, a sum he'd calculated and recalculated in his mind during the drive home.

Jessie glanced at the money, then back at him. "John, you'll need that for gas later this week."

"It's okay. We need groceries more than gas right now. I can charge gas." The words sounded practical, but inside, he was thinking that this way, at least he could feel like he was putting something on the table, even if it wasn't steak or potatoes.

He set his bag down and headed for the kitchen. "You eat dinner?"

"Yeah, we had leftovers; there's some in the fridge if you're hungry."

He wasn't hungry; he was tired and frustrated, so far past hungry that food seemed irrelevant. But he opened the fridge anyway and stared at the Tupperware containers without really seeing them.

"John?" Jessie appeared in the kitchen doorway. "We need to talk."

John felt himself tense for a moment.

Those four words again. The familiar feeling again. He closed the fridge with a soft thud and turned to face his wife. "About what?"

Jessie took a breath, and he could see her gathering courage. "Principal Morrison offered me a full-time position, starting next week. It would mean better pay, benefits..."

"Take it," he said at once.

Jessie blinked. "You don't want to talk about it?"

"What's there to talk about? We need the money, so take the job."

"John, it's not that simple. It would mean longer hours and more responsibility. I'd be home later, and you'd need to..."

"I said take it." His voice came out harder than he intended. "We need the income, end of discussion."

Jessie's eyes narrowed. "Don't do that. Don't shut me out and make unilateral decisions. This affects both of us."

"You're right," he said, his voice tight. "It affects both of us, which is why you should take the job, because I clearly can't provide for this family anymore."

"That's not what I..."

"Isn't it?" He crossed his arms. "Isn't that exactly what this is? You stepping up because I'm failing? You're becoming the bread-winner because I can't cut it?"

"John, that's not fair."

"No, what's not fair is that I worked for fifteen years, did everything right, and got thrown away like garbage, and what's not fair is that I'm delivering pizza to people I went to high school with while you have to work full-time because your husband is useless."

"Stop it." Her voice was sharp. "Stop feeling sorry for yourself and stop making this about your pride. I'm offering to take this job because it's good for our family, not because you're failing. We're supposed to be a team, remember?"

"Some team," he muttered. "One player carries the whole game while the other one rides the bench."

Jessie stared at him for a long moment, and he saw something shift in her expression: hurt giving way to frustration, frustration giving way to something harder.

"You know what? Fine, feel sorry for yourself, wallow in your pride, but I'm taking the job, John, because unlike you, I'm not going to let my ego get in the way of taking care of our children."

She turned and walked back to the living room, leaving him standing in the kitchen with his hands clenched into fists. He felt as if he had been physically slapped, and it stung. He wanted to follow her, to apologize, to explain that it was not about ego but about feeling like he had lost everything that made him who he was.

Yet the words seemed stuck in his throat, trapped behind a wall of pride and shame he had been building up for weeks.

He grabbed his keys and headed to the door.

"Where are you going?" Jessie called from the living room.

"Out," he said and left before she could say anything else.

He drove aimlessly for a while, his mind churning. Jessie was right, he knew she was right. Taking the full-time position was the smart thing to do, the practical thing, but knowing that didn't make it hurt any less. It didn't make him feel any less like a failure. He also knew that this was a stupid thing to argue about, but somehow it seemed like every discussion became an argument.

For fifteen years, he had been the provider. That was his role, his identity, his purpose. He went to work, brought home a paycheck, and took care of his family. Jessie had supported him, worked part-time, managed the home, and raised the kids. It had worked; they had been happy.

But now everything was upside down. Jessie would be working full-time while he... what? Delivered pizza, did odd jobs, stayed home with the kids? The thought made his stomach churn, not because there was anything wrong with it. He knew plenty of stay-at-home dads, and they were doing important work. But it wasn't supposed to be him. That wasn't the plan. That wasn't who he was.

Except maybe it was now. Maybe this was who John Mitchell had become: a man whose wife had to carry everything because he couldn't.

He found himself at the park again, that same playground where he'd sat a few days ago, questioning God's presence. He parked and got out, walking to the swings. He sat down on one, the chains creaking under his weight.

There was something oddly comforting about sitting on a swing, something that reached back to childhood, to a time when the biggest concern was how high you could go, how close to the sky. He remembered that feeling: the rush of air, the momentary weightlessness at the peak of each arc, the simple joy of motion. That child felt like a stranger now, someone from another lifetime. Someone who'd believed the world made sense, that good things happened to good people, that God answered prayers.

He stared up at the night sky, gripping the chains.

"I don't understand Your plan here," he said to the darkness."I don't understand what You're trying to teach me. Is this about humility? Because I'm pretty sure I've learned that lesson. Is it about trust? Because I'm trying, God. I'm really trying. But it's hard to trust when everything keeps getting worse."

A soft breeze rustled through the trees, carrying the smell of spring: new growth, fresh starts, all the things he could almost taste yet couldn't seem to find in his own life.

"Jessie says we're supposed to be a team," he continued. "And she's right. I know she's right. But it doesn't feel like a team when I'm the one failing; it feels like I'm dragging her down, like she'd be better off without me."

There it was the thought that had been creeping in more and more lately, dark and insidious. The life insurance policy would pay off the house and give them breathing room. Jessie could take the full-time job without worrying about his pride. The kids would be okay. They were young enough that they would adjust, move on, and remember him as the dad who loved them but couldn't quite make it work.

He shook his head, trying to dislodge the thought. This was crazy. He wasn't seriously considering it. No, he was just tired, overwhelmed, having dark thoughts because he was stressed and scared and didn't know how to fix any of these problems.

But the thought's didn't leave; they just settled deeper, taking root in the exhausted soil of his mind.

When he got home, it was late. The house was dark except for the porch light Jessie always left on. He let himself in quietly and found her asleep on the couch, her laptop still open beside her and papers scattered around her. She had been working, probably trying to get ahead, before the new position started.

He stood in the doorway, looking at his wife. Even in sleep, she looked tired, worry lines creasing her forehead and her hair coming loose from its ponytail. She was carrying so much: the job, the kids, the finances, and now his crisis on top of it all.

He should wake her, help her to bed, apologize for walking out, but he couldn't make himself move. Instead, he grabbed a blanket from the closet and draped it over her, careful not to wake her. Then he went down to the basement, where he belonged.

He opened his laptop, and his email inbox loaded on the screen: two new messages. His heart jumped; maybe this was it, maybe this was finally the break he needed. But they were both automated rejections: Thank you for your interest. We've decided to pursue other candidates. "God, help me find work," he whispered, but the words felt emptier than ever. How many times had he prayed that prayer? Hundreds? Thousands? And what had changed? Nothing. Absolutely nothing.

He closed the laptop and sat in the dark, listening to the house settle around him. Somewhere above Jessie was sleeping, probably dreaming of answered prayers and God's provision. Somewhere above his children were sleeping, trusting that their parents would figure this out.

Down in the basement, John Mitchell sat alone and felt the darkness pressing in. It was not just the physical darkness of the room but something deeper, heavier: the darkness of despair, of hopelessness, of a man who had run out of options and was starting to think there might be only one way out.

He pulled out his phone and opened the browser, typing before he could stop himself: life insurance policy payout.

The search results loaded: articles about beneficiaries, claim processes, and exclusions. He scrolled through them, his heart pounding. Most policies had a suicide clause: two years before they would pay out. How long had he had his policy? He couldn't remember. Eight years? Ten?

He closed the browser, his hands shaking. What was he doing? What was he thinking? This was insane. He wasn't seriously considering it.

But he was, and that was the terrifying part. He was sitting in his basement at 12:47 a.m., researching life insurance payouts, and some part of him was thinking it made sense. Some part of him was doing the math: $500,000 would pay off the house, give Jessie and the kids breathing room, and let them start over without the burden of his failure dragging them down.

"God," he whispered, his voice breaking. "Please, please help me. I don't want to think like this, I don't want to be this person, but I don't know what else to do. How do I keep going when everything feels hopeless?"

The silence that continued to answer felt like abandonment, or maybe it felt like permission. He couldn't tell anymore. He couldn't tell the difference between God's voice and his own thoughts, between faith and desperation, between hope and the absence of it.

He sat in the dark for a long time, his phone in his hands, the life insurance search still in his browser history, a secret he'd have to delete before anyone saw it, another lie to add to the growing pile.

In a few days, Jessie would accept the full-time position. Tomorrow, he would deliver more pizza, do more handyman jobs, and apply for more positions that wouldn't call back. Tomorrow he'd put on his mask and pretend everything was fine.

But tonight, in the darkness, John Mitchell admitted to himself what he'd been avoiding for weeks: he was drowning, and he was starting to think that maybe, just maybe, it would be easier to stop fighting and let himself sink. The thought should have terrified him; instead, it felt almost like relief. He felt as if an unseen presence was circling him, not with claws or teeth but with whispers that wiggled into the cracks of his thoughts. The darkness in the room seemed alive, whispering half-truths that lodged in his mind.

He had no strength left to argue with the voices, no Bible verses to recite, no prayers that felt real anymore, and not even anger to sustain him. He thought about going back upstairs, sneaking up the stairs like a thief, ever so quietly, because he did not want to have another argument with his wife and, worse still, he did not want to wake Emma or Caleb. Instead, he decided he should at least check the job boards again.

But he already knew the truth. The job boards would show the same dismal options: maintenance positions at run-down apartment complexes offering poverty wages, no benefits, and certainly no health insurance for his family. Nothing that could save his house or his family. He stared at the computer screen, refreshing the job board website in hopes that a new posting would appear, something he could apply to before anyone else. His mind kept returning to dark thoughts. He was a failure. He couldn't pay the bills. He spent too much time in the basement, hiding from his wife.

He prayed the five-word prayer again: "God, help me find work!"

Over the last few weeks, John had developed a routine, as if by following a strict schedule he could stave off the fear that he was becoming untethered from the rest of the world. He would shuffle down the stairs with a cup of coffee, log into the battered laptop, and cycle through the job boards with relentless, almost religious monotony.

There were never any answers waiting for him, only the same stale postings for jobs he had already applied to or positions that paid so little he would need three of them just to tread water. His eyes felt heavy, tired of staring at the laptop screen, hoping to see some answer appear that would bring some hope into this dark basement.

He closed the laptop and lay his head down, intending only to rest his eyes. Within moments, he slipped into a nightmare. He was running through the darkness, shadows stretching around him as faceless pursuers closed in, their echoing voices harassing him in the night: "Failure! You are a failure! Worthless!" John Mitchell ran deeper into the nightmare that his life had become.

CHAPTER 5

DECEPTION OF THE HEART

The call came on a Thursday afternoon while John was replacing a leaky faucet for a landlord in Harrisburg. He almost didn't answer; it was an unknown number, probably spam, but something made him wipe his hands on his jeans and swipe to accept.

"John Mitchell?" The voice was familiar, but he couldn't immediately place it.

"Yeah, this is John."

"Hey, man! It's Dave Martinez from Riverside."

He straightened up, his heart doing a small jump. Dave had been on the line with him for years, a good guy, someone he had genuinely liked. They had lost touch after the closure, as everyone had scattered, trying to find their footing in the wreckage.

"Dave! Hey, how are you? Did you find something?"

"Actually, yeah. That's why I'm calling." Dave's voice had an energy to it, an excitement that he hadn't heard in months. "I wanted to reach out to some of the guys from the old crew. You got a minute?"

He glanced at the sink. The woman who had hired him was upstairs, giving him space to work. "Sure, what's up?"

"So, I know things have been rough since Riverside closed. I've been there, man: couldn't find anything decent, bills piling up, the whole nightmare. But I got connected with this opportunity about a month ago, and John, it's been a game-changer."

His stomach tightened. He'd heard this tone before: the slightly too enthusiastic pitch, the vague promises, but he kept listening anyway.

"What kind of opportunity?"

"It's a business venture, investment-based. Basically, you put in some capital upfront and the returns are incredible. I'm talking 40% in the first month, and it compounds from there. I've already made back my initial investment plus another three grand."

"Dave, that sounds like..."

"I know what you're thinking," Dave interrupted. "I thought the same thing at first, but it's legit, man. It's all about cryptocurrency arbitrage, buying low on one exchange and selling high on another. The company handles all the technical stuff, so you just invest and watch it grow."

John's skepticism warred with his desperation. Forty percent returns? That was impossible, that was... but what if it wasn't? What if this was the break he'd been praying for?

"How much did you invest?" he asked, hating himself for even asking.

"I started with five grand. I know that sounds like a lot, but John, I made it back in three weeks, and now I'm reinvesting and the numbers just keep climbing. I'm telling you this is real."

Five thousand dollars. He had exactly $7,000 left in their savings account, the last buffer between them and complete financial collapse, money that had been disappearing dollar by dollar as he paid for gas and groceries and tried to keep them afloat.

"I don't know, Dave, that's a lot of money to risk."

"That's the thing: it's not really a risk. The company's been around for three years, and they've got thousands of investors. I can send you the website, testimonials, everything. Look, I wouldn't be calling if I didn't think this could help. We're all in the same boat here, and I want to see the guys from Riverside get back on their feet."

His mind was racing: forty percent returns. If he invested $5,000 and made it back plus $2,000 in a month, that would give them breathing room. He could pay the mortgage, catch up on bills, and maybe even have enough left over to stop delivering pizza and focus on finding a real job.

"Send me the information," he heard himself say. "Let me take a look at it."

"Absolutely! I'll text you the link right now, but John, one thing: they're closing this investment round at the end of the week, so if you're interested, you'll need to move fast because these opportunities don't stay open long."

Of course, the pressure tactic, the artificial urgency. Every red flag he had ever learned about waved frantically in his mind, but underneath the skepticism was something more powerful: hope, desperate, dangerous hope.

"Got it, Dave. Thanks for thinking of me."

"Hey, we're Riverside guys; we look out for each other. Check it out and let me know, because I really think this could be the answer you've been looking for."

After they hung up, he stared at his phone. A text from Dave appeared almost immediately with a link to a website, Crypto Arbitrage Solutions. The site looked professional, with a sleek design, testimonials from smiling people, and charts showing exponential growth, and he scrolled through it, his heart pounding.

"I invested $10,000 and earned $4,000 in my first month!"

"This changed my life; I was able to pay off my debt and start saving for my kids' college."

"The returns are exactly as promised, and I wish I'd found this sooner."

He clicked on the "How It Works" section. The explanation was just technical enough to sound legitimate but vague enough that he couldn't quite follow it, something about automated trading algorithms and market inefficiencies. It made his head hurt, but that didn't mean it was fake. Plenty of real things were complicated.

He should research this, ask Jessie, and pray about it.

But the deadline was Friday, and he was so tired of waiting, so tired of praying prayers that went unanswered, so tired of watching his family struggle while he failed to fix all the problems that continued to get bigger every day.

"God," he whispered, standing in this stranger's bathroom with a wrench in his hand and desperation in his chest, "if this is wrong, stop me. Please. Give me a sign, show me another way, something. But I need help. We need help. And this might be it."

The silence that answered felt like permission.

He finished the faucet repair and drove home, the numbers cycling through his head on repeat: forty percent returns, compounding investments, software that automatically placed trades at higher rates. He pulled up the website again at every red light, reading testimonials and looking for cracks in the facade, but everything looked legitimate. The company had an address in Delaware, a customer service number, and even a Better Business Bureau rating, though he noticed it was "not accredited" in small print at the bottom.

At home, he found Jessie in the kitchen making dinner. Emma was at the table doing homework, and Caleb was in the living room watching TV. It was a normal evening routine, a normal life that was all hanging by a slender thread.

"How'd the job go?" Jessie asked, without looking up from the chicken she was seasoning.

"Fine. Fixed a faucet in Harrisburg," he said, setting his toolbox by the door. "Made sixty bucks."

Sixty dollars for two hours of work and an hour of driving. It was better than pizza delivery, but it wasn't enough. House payment, car payment, insurance, groceries. The list seemed endless, and the meager few dollars a day just didn't stretch far enough. It would never be enough.

"That's good," she said, and he heard the forced optimism in her voice. She was trying so hard to stay positive, to keep believing things would work out, and here he was, keeping secrets, obsessing over something he couldn't even explain to her yet.

Once the kids were in bed, he sat in the basement with his laptop open. The Crypto Arbitrage Solutions website glowed on the screen. He'd spent the past two hours researching cryptocurrency arbitrage, and from what he could tell, it was a real thing. People really did make money exploiting price differences between exchanges, and the real question was whether this particular company was legitimate or a scam.

He opened a new tab and searched for "Crypto Arbitrage Solutions reviews."

The results were mixed. Some people raved about their returns, while others called it a Ponzi scheme. One forum post from three months ago said the company had stopped responding to withdrawal requests, but another post from last week showed someone celebrating their payout.

It was impossible to know what was real and what was not. The internet was full of people with agendas, competitors trying to tear down successful companies, and bitter investors who had made bad decisions and wanted to blame someone else.

He pulled up his bank account. $7,000. Their last safety net. If he invested $5,000 and it worked, they would have $9,000 in a month. If it did not work...

He couldn't think about that. He had to believe it would work. He had to believe that God wouldn't let him walk into a trap, that this was the answer to his prayers, that finally, *after everything that had gone wrong*, something was going to go right.

He felt out of his depth. Opening an account with Crypto Arbitrage Solutions had been straightforward enough, but then he had to buy cryptocurrency, actual crypto, and deposit it into his new account. It wasn't rocket science, but it also wasn't something he entirely understood.

"Okay," he muttered, reading the instructions again. "Buy XRP, transfer to wallet address, simple." But then he had to find a wallet, something called MetaMask, then he had to buy the XRP from a company that provided what they called a bridge to buy the crypto and then transfer it to his new MetaMask wallet. Okay, so it was not quite as easy as he thought.

XRP was supposed to be the next big thing in crypto. Thousands of people were convinced that XRP would one day be worth thousands of dollars per coin, just like Bitcoin, which is now worth over $100,000 per coin.

But it didn't feel simple. Hours of research had led him down rabbit holes of online forums where people spoke about XRP with an intensity that bordered on manic, saying, "Just buy it, you can't go wrong," and, "This is going to make people rich." The certainty in their words felt off. The warning bells should have been ringing loud and clear, but John continued on, filling out forms and agreeing to small print he didn't understand because this had to be the answer. His finger hesitated over the send button, and then a war started in his head, he could easily imagine the devil on one shoulder and the angel on the other.

Jessie doesn't need to know the details, only that it worked out.

This is insane; this is how people lose everything.

But he was already losing everything, so at this point what difference did it make?

Jessie will kill you if she finds out.

He wouldn't tell her, not yet, not until the returns came in and he could surprise her with good news for once, not until he could prove that he wasn't a complete failure, that he could still provide, that he could still fix this mess.

Pray about it first.

He closed his eyes. "God, I'm going to do this. If it's wrong, stop me: close the website, make my computer crash, something. But if You're silent, I'm taking that as a yes, and I'm taking that as You opening a door, because I've been asking for help for weeks and this is the first thing that's looked like an answer."

He waited ten seconds, then twenty. The house held its familiar quiet, the mundane sounds of home and neighborhood persisting around him, and for John there was no intervention or warning.

Nothing.

He clicked to confirm, and just like that, the money was gone, converted, transferred, committed.

There's no going back now.

Now his new investment account was funded with a crypto coin he had never heard of before.

A loading screen appeared, then a confirmation page: Thank you for your investment; your account has been funded.

This service uses AI to enter trades on your behalf using XRP, which is then converted into the best trading currency, and you can track your returns in real time through your investor dashboard. Initial processing takes 24 to 48 hours.

He stared at the screen, his heart pounding. He'd done it, he had just invested $5,000 of their last $7,000 in a company he had learned about three hours ago from a phone call that might have been too good to be true.

He felt sick, hopeful, terrified, and relieved.

"Please let this work," he whispered, "please, God, let this work."

The next morning, he woke up with a knot in his stomach. He'd barely slept, his mind spinning through scenarios. In the best case, he'd have $7,000 in a month and could start digging them out of this hole; in the worst case, he couldn't let himself think about it.

He checked his phone before getting out of bed and saw an email from Crypto Arbitrage Solutions: "Welcome to the CAS family! Your investment is being processed, and you'll see your first returns within 48 hours."

His chest loosened slightly; it was real. It was happening, and he just had to wait.

Jessie stirred beside him. "You're up early."

"Couldn't sleep," he said, and it was true.

Job search stress?

"Yeah." That was also true, in a way.

She moved toward him, her hand finding his. "It's going to be okay, John; I know it doesn't feel like it right now, but God's going to come through. He always does."

He squeezed her hand, guilt twisting in his gut. It was the same feeling as eating a questionable tuna sandwich from a convenience store, in that moment just before the sickness hits, when you know you've made a terrible mistake, but it's too late to undo it. She had no idea what he'd done, no idea that he'd bet their savings and their future on a website and a phone call from a former coworker, no idea that in forty-eight hours they would either be saved or ruined. "I hope you're right," he said.

"I am," she said, then kissed his cheek and got up to start her day, her faith intact and her trust in God unshaken.

He lay in bed for a few more minutes, staring at the ceiling and wondering if he had just made the biggest mistake of his life.

Friday passed in a blur of anxiety. He checked his phone every ten minutes, refreshing his email and logging into the investor dashboard that showed his $5,000 investment in the form of XRP coins but no returns yet, only a status that said processing and that initial returns would appear within 48 hours.

He delivered pizza that night, his mind elsewhere. He smiled at customers, thanked them for tips, and drove from house to house on autopilot, all the while distracted. All he could think about was that dashboard, those numbers, the promise of 40% returns that would save them.

Saturday morning. Still nothing. He tried to act normal, playing with the kids and helping Jessie with laundry, pretending his entire world wasn't balanced on the edge of a knife. Every time his phone buzzed, his heart jumped, but it was always something else: a delivery request, a spam email, a text from his mom asking how he was doing.

By Saturday night he was starting to panic. It had been more than 48 hours, and the website said returns would appear by then. He logged into the dashboard again: Processing.

He tried calling the customer service number, but after it rang four times it went straight to voicemail.

"You've reached Crypto Arbitrage Solutions. Our office hours are Monday through Friday from 9 a.m. to 5 p.m. Eastern, so please leave a message and we'll return your call within one business day."

He didn't leave a message; he hung up and stared at his phone, a cold dread settling in his stomach.

Sunday morning, Jessie asked if he was going to church. He said no; he had applications to work on. The truth was he couldn't sit in that building or pretend to sing songs, not while his mind churned over whether he'd made a terrible mistake. But it was too early to tell. It could still work; it just might take longer than he'd thought.

After Jess left with the kids, he sat in the basement and searched for Crypto Arbitrage Solutions again. This time, he dug deeper, past the first page of results, past the testimonials and the promotional articles.

On page three, he found a forum post from two days ago: CAS had stopped responding to withdrawal requests, and the poster wrote, "I think it's a scam."

His vision blurred. The word SCAM seemed to flash on the

screen in bright red, screaming at him: You're an idiot. Stupid. How could you be so dumb?

He clicked on the thread, hands shaking. Dozens of comments from people were saying the same thing. The website was still up, the dashboard still showed their investments, but nobody could get their money out. Customer service was not answering. One user posted that the Delaware address was just a PO box.

This was it. The final straw. The end of the rainbow, and there was no gold, no payoff, no second chance. Do not pass go, do not collect two hundred dollars. Just his own stupidity, his ignorance, his failure. All on him, all his fault.

As he read on about the crypto scam, he began to see people talking about how XRP was not actually worth more money and that it had all been hype to get more people to buy the crypto coin. He read that crypto scams work so well because once you send money and buy crypto and then send that crypto to a scam company, you cannot get that money back.

John leaned closer to the screen, his pulse hammering.

User247: Lost $15k to Crypto Arbitrage Solutions. They're ghosts now; no one answers.

A broken whisper fell from his lips. "Please... not this."

He tried calling Dave Martinez, but the call went straight to voicemail. He tried texting, *"Hey man, have you been able to withdraw any money from CAS?"*

No response.

He pulled up his bank account. The $5,000 was gone, just like he'd authorized, and it wasn't coming back.

He'd been scammed. He'd taken their last $5,000, invested it in a Ponzi scheme, and now it was gone, just gone.

Vanished into the digital ether, it was stolen by people who had built a professional-looking website and hired someone to make phone calls to desperate idiots like John Mitchell.

"God," he said, his voice shaking, "I asked You to stop me. I asked You for a sign. Why didn't You stop me?"

But he knew the answer. God had been silent, and he had taken that silence as permission. He had wanted so badly to believe in a miracle that he had ignored every red flag, every warning sign, every instinct that told him this was too good to be true.

And now they were ruined, completely, totally, irreversibly ruined. He hadn't just failed; he had destroyed his life, obliterating any chance he had to somehow pull out of this pit he had so willingly jumped into.

He sat in the basement, staring at the bank account balance. How much was actually left? He tried to calculate: $1,789. No, wait, they had just made the car payment.

His mind scrambled through the numbers: the electric bill was due, groceries, gas to keep looking for work.

And then, with cold, crushing certainty, he knew there wouldn't be enough for the mortgage payment.

Something broke inside him.

A final breaking, the last piece of hope crumbling into dust.

He'd failed. He'd failed his family, failed to provide, failed to protect them, and now, because of his desperation and his pride and his refusal to tell Jessie what he was doing, he'd made everything infinitely worse.

The mortgage was due in two weeks. There was less than $1,800 left. The payment was $1,200, which left what, $500? Maybe $400 after the other bills cleared, for food, utilities, gas, everything else. And after that, they would have nothing.

He pulled up his email and found the payment-due notice they'd received last week. He'd hidden it from Jessie, telling himself he'd figure something out before it became real, but now it was real, now it was inevitable.

Final notice: Payment must be received within 30 days or foreclosure proceedings will begin.

Thirty days. They had thirty days before they would lose the house.

His phone buzzed. A text from Jessie: *Service is over, taking the kids for ice cream, home around 1:30.*

He stared at the message. In a few hours Jessie would come home with the kids, and he would have to look her in the eye and pretend everything was fine. He would have to smile and ask about church and act like he had not just destroyed their future.

Or he could tell her, confess what he'd done, face her anger and disappointment, and figure out together what to do next.

But he couldn't make himself do it, couldn't make himself admit that he'd been so stupid, so desperate, so willing to believe in a miracle that he'd walked straight into a trap.

He deleted the Crypto Arbitrage Solutions emails, cleared his browser history, and removed any evidence that he'd ever heard of the company. Then he went upstairs and made himself a sandwich he couldn't eat, waiting for his family to come home, waiting to put on another mask and tell another lie.

Because that was what John Mitchell had become: a man who lied to the people he loved, who made catastrophic decisions in secret, who was so far gone that he couldn't even ask for help anymore.

This was his fault, all of it. Where was it in the Bible? Jeremiah, he thought. "The heart is deceitful above all things, and desperately wicked: who can know it?" He remembered that verse from vacation bible school because of a contest to memorize bible verses.

He knew it. Yes, he knew it now, and soon Jessie would too.

Desperation clawed at his mind, tearing relentlessly at the last shred of his sanity.

He had allowed his own heart to deceive him. Dave Martinez would have some explaining to do, sure, but in the end, he was the one who pressed that button. His decision. His stupidity. His fault. The sandwich sat untouched on the plate. The clock ticked toward 1:00 p.m. He sat at the kitchen table, staring at Emma's drawing on the fridge, "God keeps His promises," and wondered if God had kept His promise to let John destroy himself.

Because that's what it felt like, like God had been silent, not because He was absent but because He was letting John make his own choices. And John had chosen poorly, catastrophically.

As Samson had allowed his heart to be deceived, John now understood how easy it could be to make a fatal mistake.

CHAPTER 6

THE VALUE OF A LIFE

John stopped praying on a Monday. It was not a conscious decision. There was no declaration; he just forgot to pray. He woke up, went through his morning routine, and realized he hadn't said the five words, God, help me find work, that had become his desperate mantra. And he felt nothing. No guilt. No conviction. Just a hollow emptiness where faith once lived.

It had been three days since he'd discovered the scam, three days of carrying the secret like a stone around his neck, three days of looking Jessie in the eye and lying about why he seemed distracted, why he couldn't sleep, why he kept checking his phone.

A late payment notice had come in the mail; there were no more emails. The notice had demanded payment in thirty days or else. The threatening letter sat in the glove compartment of his truck, hidden from Jessie along with everything else. Twenty-seven days until they lost the house. Twenty-seven days until his failure became public, undeniable, complete.

He was seated at the kitchen table, coffee growing cold in his hands, staring at nothing. Jessie had already left for work, her new part-time position at the restaurant starting today. They had argued about it last night. He had been against her taking yet another job, but she had said they no longer had a choice. Now, instead of having a day off, she would be working at another job just to make a few extra dollars.

She was trying to do too much, finding time to work part-time between her full-time job responsibilities whenever she had a chance to make extra cash. Any time she could find 8 hours in the week where she might get a shift to make extra money.

Emma and Caleb were at school, and the house was silent except for the sound of the refrigerator running and the clock's relentless ticking.

He should be applying for jobs and sending out resumes. He should be figuring out how to tell Jessie about the money he had lost, about how he'd thrown it all away on a sure thing that turned out to be a scam. He should be doing something, anything, to fix this, to patch up the damage and prove he was not completely hopeless.

Instead, he sat motionless, feeling the weight of his choices pressing down on him like the depths of water, as if he were sinking deeper and deeper into an ocean with no bottom.

His phone buzzed as a text from Jessie came in: *Day is going great! The kids will be with your mom after school, so don't forget to pick them up by 6 Love you!*

He stared at the message. His mom. He'd forgotten Jessie had arranged that, which meant he had the whole day alone. No deliveries scheduled, no handyman jobs lined up, just him and the silence and the growing certainty that there was no way out of this.

He typed back, "Sounds good. Love you too."

Another lie, or maybe not a lie. He did love her, but the words felt empty. Like everything else, something was missing something vital that had vanished along with his job.

He set the phone down and looked around the kitchen. This

was the house they'd bought eight years ago, stretching their budget and believing in a future that now seemed like it was never going to materialize. Emma's drawings were on the fridge, Caleb's spelling test with a gold star was beside them, and the coffee maker Jessie's parents had given them for Christmas sat on the counter, all the pieces of a normal life that he had destroyed.

He got up and walked to the basement, his feet carrying him down the narrow stairs as they had a hundred times before, yet this time it felt different, heavier, as if each step echoed a quiet certainty. This time felt final, as if the air itself had gone still around him and there was no longer any real hope left, only the lingering awareness that something important had already slipped away.

The basement was cool and dim, lit only by the small window near the ceiling. His makeshift office sat in the corner with a folding table, a chair, his laptop, and a filing cabinet where he kept important documents.

He opened the bottom drawer and pulled out a manila folder labeled "Insurance."

Inside was their life insurance policy. He had gotten it when Emma was born, back when he was still thinking about the future and still planning for contingencies. It provided $500,000 in coverage, enough to pay off the house, cover the kids' education, and give Jessie breathing room to rebuild.

He had looked at the suicide clause last week, that night in the basement when the dark thoughts first started taking shape: a two-year waiting period. He'd had the policy for eleven years, so it would pay out.

He set the folder on the desk and stared at it. This was insane. He was sitting in his basement, looking at his life insurance policy and doing the math on how much his death was worth. This wasn't him. This wasn't who John Mitchell was.

But even as he said it, he knew he was lying, because the thought had been there for weeks now, growing stronger and more insistent. And now, with the scam and the foreclosure and the complete absence of any other option, it didn't feel like a dark impulse anymore. It felt like the only rational choice left.

His family would be devastated; he knew that. Emma and Caleb would grow up without a father. Jessie would have to explain to them why Daddy wasn't coming home. They would cry and hurt and wonder if they could have done something to save him.

But they'd also have a house, they'd have money, and they'd have a future that didn't include his failure dragging them down. In time, they'd be okay, better than okay, better than they'd ever be with him.

Better off without him. He closed the folder and put it back in the drawer, but not yet, because he wasn't ready yet, though soon, maybe, probably.

He climbed the stairs and grabbed his keys. He needed to get out of this house, away from these thoughts, away from all of his mistakes.

He drove away, his mind numb. He passed the closed factory, the church, and the elementary school. All the landmarks of his life, all the places that used to mean something. Now they were just buildings, just geography, just reminders of everything he'd lost.

He ended up at Walmart, though he couldn't remember deciding to go there or even turning down the familiar streets. He parked and sat in the truck, staring at the entrance with a dull, unfocused gaze. People came and went, mothers with toddlers tugging at their hands, elderly couples leaning on each other for balance, teenagers laughing at something on their phones and shoving one another playfully. Normal people living normal lives, unburdened by the heavy weight he carried in his heart and the constant noise going on in his head.

He went inside, moving through the aisles on autopilot. He wasn't shopping for anything specific; he was just moving, just existing, just trying to outrun the thoughts that followed him everywhere.

In the sporting goods section, he stopped. Behind the glass counter, locked away, were the guns: rifles and shotguns. He stared at them, his heart pounding.

His father had owned a revolver, a .38 Special kept in a lockbox in the bedroom closet. After his father died five years ago, he inherited it. He put it in the basement, in the same filing cabinet where he kept the insurance policy, and hadn't thought about it since.

Until now.

"Can I help you with something?" a young employee appeared beside him, wearing a blue vest and a name tag that said "Brandon."

His mouth was dry. "No, just looking."

"Let me know if you need anything," Brandon said with a smile as he walked away.

He stood there for another moment, staring at the guns behind the glass. Then he turned and walked quickly toward the exit, his hands shaking, his breath coming too fast.

In the truck, he gripped the steering wheel and tried to calm down. This was crazy; he was crazy. He needed help. He needed to talk to someone, to tell Jessie everything, to stop carrying this alone.

But he couldn't. He couldn't face her disappointment, her anger, her realization that she had married a man who was fundamentally broken. He couldn't watch her try to fix him, try to have enough faith for both of them, or try to hold together a family that he had destroyed.

It would be easier for everyone if he were not here anymore.

He started the truck and drove home, the thought settling over him like a blanket, not comforting exactly but familiar, expected, almost peaceful in its finality.

At home, he went straight to the basement. He opened the

filing cabinet and pulled out the lockbox. He entered the combination and the lock box clicked open.

The box had belonged to his father.

Inside was the revolver, exactly as he remembered it: dark metal, wooden grip, heavier than it looked. His father had taught him to shoot when he was sixteen, taking him to a range outside town and showing him how to hold it, how to aim, how to respect the weapon's power.

"A gun is a tool," his father had said. "It's not good or evil. It's what you use it for that matters."

He picked up the revolver and felt its weight in his hand. What was he doing? What was he planning to do?

He opened his laptop, the screen's glow harsh in the dim basement light.

He navigated to the crypto exchange website, his hands trembling as he typed in his login credentials.

The page loaded. His account balance stared back at him, still showing "pending." But he understood now. It would stay pending forever. The site was fake, the balance a lie, his money really gone, and there was nothing he could do about it.

He minimized the browser window and stared at the Google search bar, his fingers moving almost on their own as he typed: *life insurance suicide clause*.

He clicked the first result. Two years: the policy would pay out after that time.

Nothing had changed about that either, he thought; he was stuck, and there was no way out.

He had, after all, chosen to invest in a scam.

His eyes drifted down the search results, and a headline caught his attention: Suicide Statistics United States, CDC.

He clicked it.

The first line stopped him cold: *one death every 11 minutes*.

"That can't be right," he muttered as he leaned closer to the screen.

But it was. Last year, over 49,000 people ended their lives, one death every 11 minutes.

He kept scrolling. Suicide was among the top eight leading causes of death for people ages 10 to 64 and was the second leading cause of death for people ages 10 to 34.

"Kids," he whispered aloud, children as young as 10.

The statistics kept coming, each one landing with a sickening weight.

5.5% of adults age 18 and older in the United States had serious thoughts about suicide in 2024, and the prevalence was highest among young adults age 18 to 25 at 12.6%.

In 2024, 14.3 million adults reported having serious thoughts of suicide, and 2.2 million adults attempted suicide during the past year.

At the bottom of the page, bold text caught his eye:

If you or someone you know is struggling or having thoughts of suicide, call or text 988.

Three numbers.

Below it, more information: *The 988 Suicide & Crisis Lifeline is a national network of more than 200 crisis centers that provides 24/7 confidential support to people in suicidal, mental health, and substance misuse crises.*

Veterans can press "1" after dialing 988 to connect directly to the Veterans Crisis Lifeline.

He knew this was a horrible thing to even think about, and he knew something else: it was a sin.

His mind drifted to Bible verses he'd heard over the years. There were a lot of them, he was sure, though he couldn't remember them: Sunday school lessons from childhood, sermons he'd half listened to. But one came through loud and clear, embedded in his memory from countless repetitions.

The Ten Commandments: *Thou shalt not kill.*

Taking your own life would be a sin, murder, even if the victim is yourself.

His phone buzzed, a small vibration against his palm. A text from his mom lit the screen: *Kids are having a great time! Caleb beat me at Go Fish three times. See you at 6!*

He stared at the message, then at the gun, then back at the glowing words. His kids. His mother. His wife. All the people who loved him, who needed him, who would be quietly shattered if he did what he was thinking about doing.

But they would also be free, free from his failure, his quiet lies, his inability to provide or protect or be the man they deserved.

He put the gun back in the lockbox and closed it. Not yet. He wasn't ready yet, but he left the box on the desk instead of putting it back in the filing cabinet, just in case, just to have the option.

He went upstairs and made himself lunch, which he did not eat. He sat on the couch and turned on the TV, watching without seeing, his mind elsewhere. The afternoon passed in a blur, time moving forward as he stayed frozen.

At 5:45, he drove to his mother's house to pick up the kids. She lived ten minutes away in a small ranch house she had bought after his father died. The yard was neat, the flower beds tended, everything in its place. His mother had always been good at maintaining order, at keeping things together even when they were falling apart.

Emma and Caleb ran out when they saw his truck, their faces bright with the uncomplicated joy of children who did not know their father was drowning in debt and despair, unaware that he was getting closer to the edge every day.

"Dad! Grandma made cookies!" Caleb climbed into the back seat, already talking about his day.

Emma was quieter, studying his face as she buckled her seatbelt. "Are you okay, Dad? You look tired."

"I'm fine, sweetheart, just a long day."

His mother appeared in the doorway, waving. He waved back

and pulled out of the driveway before she could come over and ask questions he couldn't answer.

On the drive home, Caleb chattered about the cookies, the games, and how Grandma let him watch an extra episode of his favorite show. Emma was silent, occasionally glancing at him with those too-perceptive eyes.

"Dad?" she said finally. "Can I ask you something?"

"Sure, honey."

"Are you and Mom going to get a divorce?"

He swallowed, his throat suddenly tight. "What? No. Why would you think that?"

"Because you're sad all the time, and you and Mom argue a lot, and I've heard her crying more than once."

The realization settled over him with an uncomfortable silence. Jessie had been crying because of him, because he was failing her in every possible way.

"Mom and I are fine," he lied. "We're just going through a hard time right now, but we love each other, and we love you guys. That's not going to change."

Emma nodded, but she did not look convinced. "Okay."

The rest of the drive passed in silence. He pulled into their driveway just as Jessie was getting home from work. She looked exhausted, but she smiled when she saw them.

"There's my family!" She hugged the kids as they piled out of the truck. "How was Grandma's?"

"She made cookies!" Caleb announced.

"Did you save any for me?"

"Maybe one or two," Emma said, smiling for the first time since they had left.

Jessie stared at him over the kids' heads. "How was your day?"

"Fine," he said. "Quiet."

"Did you apply for anything?"

"A few things," another lie.

They went inside, and Jessie started making dinner while the kids did homework. He sat at the kitchen table, watching his family move through their evening routine and feeling like a ghost haunting his own life.

He walked over to the window overlooking the overgrown backyard. A tangled garden of wild weeds climbed the fence, choking out the honeysuckle at the edge of the trees and the fence that separated his yard from his nearest neighbor. He stared at the chaos outside and recognized something of himself in it. The weeds had not appeared overnight. They had grown slowly, almost imperceptibly, until one day the yard was unrecognizable, strangled by what he had neglected to tend, just like his own life.

He had let things slip. Small decisions had compounded into larger ones, and missed opportunities had become patterns. Now, looking at the mess he had created in this yard, he understood that he had created an equal mess within himself, a tangled chaos of his own making.

After dinner, once the kids were sleeping, Jessie found him in the living room, staring at the TV without really watching.

"John, we need to talk," she said, her voice low.

Jessie sat beside him, her face drawn and serious. "We need to have a conversation about us, about what's happening. You have been pulling away for weeks, and I don't know how to reach you anymore."

"I'm just stressed about job hunting."

"It's more than that," she said, taking his hand. "You've stopped praying with me, you barely talk to the kids, you're here but not really here, and I'm scared, John, scared I'm going to lose you."

He wanted to tell her everything, every secret he had been hiding for months: the scam, the foreclosure, the gun in the basement, the dark thoughts that would not leave him alone or let him sleep. He wanted to break down and cry, to let her hold him tightly and tell him it would all be okay, that he was not a monster and that he was not beyond saving.

But he couldn't, because it would not be okay, not really okay, since he had made it impossible for things to ever be okay again, no matter how hard he tried to fix it, no matter how many apologies he offered, or how many times he replayed it in his mind.

"I'm fine," he said, pulling his hand away, "I'm just tired."

"John..."

"I said I'm fine." He heard the edge in his voice and couldn't soften it. "Can we just not do this right now?"

Jessie stared at him for a long moment, hurt and frustration warring in her eyes. Then she stood. "Fine. But we can't keep avoiding this forever."

She went upstairs, and he heard their bedroom door close.

He sat alone in the living room, the TV flickering in the darkness, and felt the last threads connecting him to his life begin to fray. He was losing Jessie. He had already lost himself. And soon, he would lose everything else.

Maybe it was time to stop fighting, to finally just give up and let the suffocating darkness have its way.

That night, he couldn't sleep. He lay in bed beside her, listening to her breathe, wondering if she was really asleep or just pretending, wondering if she knew how close he was to the edge, wondering if she would care when he finally fell, not that he was passively slipping.

He had climbed this dangerous cliff himself, hand over hand up the steep jagged rock, ignoring every warning sign and every warning from below. Now gravity was doing its work with cold efficiency. After all, it was not the fall that got you, it was the sudden stop at the bottom, the brutal impact that turned into stillness. He allowed himself a snort of derision at the dark humor, a bitter little sound in the back of his throat, but it was not really funny at all, not with the ground rushing up to meet him.

At 2:00 a.m., he gave up and went down to the basement, where the lockbox sat on the desk where he had left it.

He opened it and took out the revolver again, feeling its weight, its solidity, its promise of an ending.

He checked the cylinder. Empty. The bullets were in a small box at the bottom of the lockbox, six rounds, more than enough.

He did not load the gun. He just held it, turning it over in his hands, getting used to the feel of it, imagining how it would be: quick, final, no more pain, no more failure, no more drowning.

His phone buzzed on the desk, a text from Jessie sent an hour ago: *I love you. Please talk to me. Whatever it is, we can face it together.*

He stared at the message, then at the gun in his hands, together. She still believed they could face things together. She still had faith in him, in them, in God's ability to fix this.

But he did not. He had run out of faith weeks ago, and now he was running out of reasons to keep going.

He put the gun back in the lockbox but left it unlocked. Then he climbed the stairs and stood in the doorway of Emma's room, watching her sleep. She looked so peaceful, so innocent, so unaware of how badly her father had failed her.

"I'm sorry," he whispered. "I'm so sorry."

He moved to Caleb's room next. His son was sprawled across the bed, one arm hanging off the side, his stuffed dinosaur clutched in the other hand. Seven years old, still believing the world was good, that his dad could fix anything, that everything would be okay.

"I love you, buddy," he said quietly. "I hope you know that."

Finally, he went to his own bedroom. Jessie was curled on her side, her face peaceful in sleep. She had probably cried herself to sleep, he realized as he saw the dried tear tracks on her cheeks in the moonlight filling the room.

He stood there for a long time, memorizing her face, trying to remember what it felt like to be the man she had married, the man who had promised to love her and protect her and be there for her always.

That man was gone. In his place was this hollow shell, this

failure, this coward who was seriously considering leaving his family because he couldn't face his own mistakes.

Again, he wondered why everything seemed so dark. Everywhere he went, from the basement to the narrow hallways, shadows pressed in like a slow, incoming tide, or maybe it was not the house at all, maybe it was just him, his thoughts, and his feelings, everything his life had quietly become.

Darkness followed him like a second shadow, or maybe he carried it inside him. Looming over all of it was the terrible certainty that Jessie would soon know. She would discover how he had betrayed them, how he had foolishly gambled away their only chance to survive, to save the home they had fought for. That secret was a time bomb, and he could feel the seconds ticking down.

He climbed into bed and stared at the ceiling, watching the shadows shift as cars passed outside. He thought about the gun in the basement, he thought about the insurance policy, and he thought about how much easier everything would be if he were not here anymore.

And for the first time, the thought did not scare him; it comforted him, like a solution finally presenting itself after months of impossible problems.

Not tonight. He was not ready tonight, but soon, maybe tomorrow, maybe the day after, but soon.

Because John Mitchell had finally accepted what he had been avoiding for weeks: he was done. Done fighting, done failing, done pretending he could fix this, done with all of it.

The decision settled over him like peace, or maybe it was just exhaustion; he couldn't tell the difference.

He closed his eyes and waited for morning, knowing that when it came, he would be one day closer to the end.

CHAPTER 7

PRAYER WARRIORS

Jessie Mitchell knew her husband was slipping away, and she felt it in the quiet pauses between their conversations and in the distant look that lingered in his eyes.

Not just physically, but spiritually and emotionally, in all the quiet ways that mattered most. She could see it in the way he moved through their house like a ghost, in the way he had stopped praying with her at night, stopped fighting for the small things that once mattered, stopped being present even when he was standing right in front of her, close enough to touch yet impossibly far away.

She had tried everything: encouragement, scripture, prayer, patience, confrontation, each one offered like a lifeline. Nothing reached him. It was like watching someone drown in slow motion, his hand slipping slowly beneath the surface every day, and no matter how desperately she reached, stretching and trembling, she couldn't seem to get to him.

Tuesday morning, Jessie sat in her car in the school parking lot, her hands gripping the steering wheel as she tried to keep herself together before going inside. She had cried herself to sleep again last night after he had shut her out. She had lain awake in the darkness once more, feeling him tense and distant beside her. When she had tried to reach for him this morning, he had pulled away with mumbled excuses, something he had been doing more often. He was not fine; he was the opposite of fine, and Jessie was terrified that she was running out of time to save him.

Her phone buzzed. A text from Rachel Kim, her best friend and prayer partner: *Coffee after work? I am worried about you.*

She stared at the message, tears blurring her vision. There was no way Rachel could have known. They had not spoken in days, but that was Rachel. She prayed constantly, listened to that still, small voice, and had an uncanny way of reaching out at exactly the right moment. It should not have surprised her anymore, but it did.

She had been trying to hold it together, to be strong, to have enough faith for both of them, but she was exhausted. She was scared, and she needed help.

She typed back, "Yes, please. I need to talk."

Rachel responded immediately, "Scoops at 4? I'll bring tissues."

Despite everything, she smiled, because Rachel always knew exactly what she needed.

She wiped her eyes, checked her makeup in the rearview mirror, and headed into the school. She had a job to do, kids to help, a life to maintain even while her own was falling apart, so she put on her professional face and walked through those doors, carrying her fear but determined to overcome it.

The day passed in a steady rhythm of lesson plans, student questions, and administrative tasks.

She moved through it on autopilot, smiling when appropriate and helping where needed, all while her mind spun with worry about John.

At 4:15, she pulled into the parking lot of Scoops, the ice cream shop where she and Rachel had been meeting for years. Rachel's minivan was already there. Through the window, she could see her friend at their usual table, two cups of coffee waiting.

Jessie took a deep breath, then went inside.

Rachel noticed her the moment she walked in and rose from her seat, concern already softening her expression. "Oh, honey," she murmured, stepping forward and pulling Jessie into a tight hug. That was all it took, Jessie broke.

She cried into Rachel's shoulder while her friend held her, saying nothing, just staying with her in the moment. The other customers in the shop politely looked away, giving them a little privacy.

After a while, Jessie drew back, accepting the tissues Rachel offered. "I'm sorry, I'm such a mess."

"You're not a mess, you're just scared. Tell me what is happening."

They sat down, and Jessie wrapped her hands around the coffee cup, needing something to hold onto. "It's John. He is... Rachel, I think I'm losing him."

"What do you mean?"

"He's given up on the job search, on us, on God. He will not talk to me, he barely talks to the kids. He's just... gone, like he's checked out even though he's still here," her voice broke. "And I do not know what to do. I have tried everything: prayer, encouragement, giving him space, confronting him. Nothing works, he just keeps pulling further away."

Rachel reached across the table and took her hand. "How long has this been going on?"

"It started when he lost his job, but it has gotten so much worse in the past few weeks. He is different, Rachel. There is something in his eyes that scares me, like he has made some decision and he is just waiting for the right moment to tell me."

"Have you talked to Pastor Mike?"

Jessie shook her head. "I did not want to betray John's privacy; he would be so angry if he knew I was talking about this."

"Jessie." Rachel's voice was gentle but firm. "This is bigger than privacy. If you think John is in real trouble, you need to get help; you cannot carry this alone."

"I know. I just... I keep thinking if I pray hard enough, if I have enough faith, God will fix this, but nothing is changing. If anything, it is getting worse." She wiped her eyes. "What if my faith is not strong enough? What if I am failing him?"

"Stop." Rachel squeezed her hand. "You're not failing him. You're doing everything you can, but Jessie, You're not God. You cannot save John, only God can do that, and sometimes God works through other people, through community, through the church."

She knew Rachel was right. She had been trying to be John's savior, trying to have enough faith for both of them, trying to fix what only God could fix, and in the process, she had been carrying a weight she was never meant to carry alone.

"I am scared," she whispered. "I am scared of what he might do. I'm scared I am going to wake up one morning, and he will be gone, and I'm scared that I'm not praying the right way or believing hard enough or..."

"Jessie, listen to me." Rachel's voice was intense. "God hears you. He sees what is happening, and He loves John even more than you do."

Jessie looked up, her eyes red from crying. "What do you mean, more than I do? I love John with everything I have."

Rachel reached across the table and took her hand. "I know you do, but think about it, Jessie. You love John more than you can express in words, right? You would do anything for him."

Jessie nodded, her throat tightening.

"Jesus loved John so much that he gave his life so that John could be free," Rachel said softly. "He died on the cross for John. For when we were yet without strength, in due time Christ died for the ungodly. That is Romans 5:6. Jesus did not just say he loved John; he proved it with his blood. That is a love deeper than anything we can fully comprehend."

She sat still, letting the words sink in. She had never thought about it like that before. The magnitude of that sacrifice, the completeness of that love, made her own devotion seem small by comparison. Her love for John was deep and sincere, but it could not match the love offered up at the cross.

"So what do we do?" she whispered.

Rachel's grip tightened. "We need to mobilize, we need to get the church praying, and we need to surround John with prayer coverage so thick that the enemy cannot get through."

"The enemy?"

Jessie had never thought of it that way. She had been so focused on the practical problems, the job loss, the money, the stress, that she had not considered the spiritual battle happening beneath the surface.

"What do I do?" she asked.

"First, we tell Pastor Mike tonight, he needs to know what is happening so he can help. Second, we gather the prayer warriors, and we get people praying around the clock. Third, you stop trying to carry this alone, you let the body of Christ do what it is designed to do, bear one another's burdens."

Jessie nodded, feeling something beginning to change inside her, not relief exactly but a loosening of the crushing weight she had been carrying. She did not have to do this alone. She was not supposed to do this alone.

"Okay," she said, "let's call Pastor Mike."

She pulled out her phone and dialed the pastor's number, her hands still trembling. She knew pastors were accustomed to emergency calls, phone calls that came at all hours when someone's world was falling apart.

"Jessie, is everything okay?"

"No," she said, her voice shaking. "I need help. It's John. Can you meet with me tonight?"

"Of course, where are you?"

"Scoops with Rachel."

"I will be right there. Thomas Avery, our youth minister, is here with me, and I would like to bring him if that is alright."

"Please," Jessie said, relief washing over her.

"I will be right there." A few minutes later, Pastor Mike and Thomas Avery walked through the door.

The pastor was in his early forties, with kind eyes and the calm presence of someone who had walked through crisis with many families. Thomas Avery, a friendly-looking man in his early thirties with dark brown hair, was dressed casually and moved to the side of the table with a reassuring smile.

Mike took a seat at the table beside Rachel, his face serious and intent.

"Tell me what is happening," he said.

She told him everything: the job loss, the way he had shut everyone out, the way he had stopped praying, the fear that something terrible was coming. She told him about the fights, the silence, the way he did not seem like himself anymore.

He listened without interrupting, his expression growing more concerned with every word. When she finished, he was quiet for a moment, his hands folded on the table.

"Jessie," he said finally, "I need to ask you something, and I need you to be honest. Do you think John might try to harm himself?"

The question hung in the air like a bomb. She had been dancing around it for days, afraid to name the fear that kept her awake at night. Now, hearing it spoken aloud, she couldn't avoid it anymore.

"I don't know," she whispered. "Maybe. I'm afraid that he might."

He nodded slowly. "Okay. Here is what we are going to do. First, I'm going to try to talk to John. He might not want to see me, but I'm going to try." He glanced at the youth minister beside him. "You know Thomas, right?"

Jessie nodded.

"Good. Thomas, can you start getting a list of our prayer warriors together? We need to set up 24-hour prayer coverage, get people signed up for shifts so someone will be praying for John every single hour."

Thomas pulled out his phone. "I am on it, Pastor."

"Every hour?" Jessie asked.

"Every hour," he confirmed. "We are going to surround him with prayer so constant, so fervent, that John will never be alone. God will meet him in every moment. And third, we are going to trust God, not because we understand what He is doing, but because we know who He is."

She felt tears streaming down her face again. "What if it is not enough? What if we pray and God does not answer?"

He slid his Bible closer to her, his hand resting on it. "God always answers, Jessie. Sometimes the answer is yes, sometimes it is no, and sometimes it is wait, but He always hears, and I believe, I truly believe, that God is going to move in John's life. I do not know how or when, but I believe that it will happen."

"I want to believe that," she said, "but I'm so tired. I have been praying for weeks, and nothing has changed."

"Then let us pray with you," Rachel said. "Let us carry this burden together."

He nodded. "Right now. Right here. Let's pray."

Jessie's eyes swept across the Scoops restaurant, couples sharing sundaes, a businessman hunched over his laptop with an espresso, and teenagers laughing over milkshakes. An elderly man stood near the door. Her chest tightened. There it was again, that familiar flutter of self-consciousness, the invisible wall she would have to push through. Praying in public. She had done it countless times since childhood, that simple act of bowing her head before a meal, but it never got easier.

Each time required the same small act of courage, choosing faithfulness over the fear of being watched, of standing out, of being labeled. She drew in a quiet breath and lowered her head.

They joined hands across the table, and they began to pray, not a polite, careful prayer but a desperate, fervent plea for God to intervene in John's life.

"Father God, we come to You in desperation. John Mitchell is in trouble. He is in trouble, and we cannot reach him, but you can. You see him. You know exactly where he is and what he is thinking, and we are asking You, we are calling on You, to reach down and grab hold of him before it is too late."

"Lord, we bind the enemy's lies in Jesus' name. We know that John Mitchell is your child, loved and valued and precious, and we ask You to break through the power of depression and despair. We pray that the supernatural power of Jesus Christ will preserve his life and free him from the power of the enemy. Lord, we pray life over him, life and hope and a future."

Jessie tried to pray, but all that came out was a sob. "Please, God. Please save my husband. Please do not let me lose him. Please."

And then, something amazing began to happen.

Jessie felt a hand on her shoulder, warm, gentle. She opened her eyes to see Margaret Chen, one of the church elders, standing beside their table. Margaret's husband, Dr. Chen, stood behind her, his hand already extended toward the table.

"We're praying with you," Margaret said softly.

From across the room, Tom Morrison and his wife, Linda, the school principal, rose from their table and moved closer. Linda's eyes were already glistening with tears." John Mitchell is family," she said. "We're not letting you fight this alone."

A young couple Jessie recognized from the contemporary service approached, then another family with two teenagers. Within moments, a circle had formed around their table. Eight, ten, twelve people, some from the church, some who'd simply been moved by the raw desperation in their prayers.

The pastor's voice grew stronger, more authoritative. "Father, we stand together as Your body, as Your church. We lift John Mitchell, a man many of us have known for years. A good man, a faithful man, who's lost his way in the darkness."

"Lord, bring him home," Tom Morrison prayed, his deep voice steady.

"Surround him with Your presence," Margaret added.

"Break through the lies he's believing," Dr. Chen said.

The voices layered over each other, some praying aloud, some whispering, some simply standing with hands extended in silent intercession. The teenage girl was crying. The young husband had his arm around his wife, both of them praying with closed eyes. An elderly man she did not recognize stood at the edge of the circle, his weathered hands raised toward heaven. His silver hair blazed in the light, as though touched by something beyond the room.

She looked around at all these faces, some familiar, some strangers, all united in this moment, all fighting for her husband. The weight she had been carrying for months began to lift, not because the situation had changed, but because she finally understood that she was not meant to carry it alone. This was what the body of Christ looked like. This was what it meant to bear one another's burdens.

For the first time in months, she felt something she had almost forgotten: peace, not just the absence of fear but the presence of something greater. John 4:18 whispered through her mind: "There is no fear in love; but perfect love casts out fear: because fear hath torment. He that feareth is not made perfect in love." In this moment, she understood she was not alone, John was not alone, God was moving among these ordinary people in this ordinary ice cream shop on an ordinary Tuesday evening.

They prayed for twenty minutes, their voices rising and falling, sometimes in unison, sometimes taking turns, and when they finally said amen, the circle remained for a moment longer, hands still touching, hearts still connected, before slowly dispersing back to their tables.

Jessie sat in the center of it all, tears streaming down her face, but for the first time, they were not tears of desperation. They were tears of gratitude, of wonder, of a burden finally shared.

"Thank you," she whispered, looking around at the faces, some returning to their tables, some lingering to squeeze her hand or offer a word of encouragement. "Thank you all."

She turned looking for the man whose silver hair had seemed to burn with its own light, but he had already left.

"This is just the beginning," Pastor Mike said. "Thomas and I will be working on getting our prayer warriors organized and praying in shifts. By tomorrow morning, we will have a full prayer schedule set up, and Jessie, I want you to call me if anything changes, day or night. If You're worried, if something feels wrong, you call me immediately, okay?"

She nodded. "Okay."

"And one more thing," He added, "do not give up hope. I know it's hard. I know You're exhausted, but God is not done with John Mitchell. This story is not over yet."

That night, after the kids were in bed, she knelt beside her bed and prayed. Her heart was quiet, no frantic pleas, no racing thoughts. Instead, she lifted up prayers of surrender, of trust, of peace. She asked for gentleness in her unrest, clarity where there had been confusion, the presence of something greater than her fears. She prayed for love that would cast out all fear, for courage in her weakness, for assurance that she and John were never alone. And in that stillness, she felt faith waking, soft but undeniable.

Father, I can't save John. I've been trying, and I can't do it. So I'm giving him to You. Completely. Fully. I'm trusting that You love him more than I do, that You have a plan I can't see, that

You're working even when I can't feel it. Please, God, pursue him. Meet him in the darkness. Lead him home.

She stayed on her knees for a long time, praying and crying and releasing the burden she'd been carrying for so long. And somewhere in the middle of that prayer, she felt something change. A deep, quiet peace rose from within her, solid and unmistakable.

God was going to move. She didn't know how or when, but He was going to move.

Jessie climbed into bed and looked at John's side, empty again, the basement light near the stairs visible under the door. She wanted to go down there, to beg him to talk to her, to tell her what was wrong. But something held her back. A sense that this was God's battle now, not hers.

She picked up her phone and texted Rachel: Thank you for today. I needed that more than you know.

Rachel responded right away: *That's what sisters in Christ do. I've got you on the emergency prayer chain. I'm praying for you right now. And I'll be praying at 2 a.m. when it's my shift.*

She smiled through her tears. She wasn't alone. She had Rachel, Pastor Mike, and soon, an army of prayer warriors standing with her.

And most importantly, she had God, the same God who had parted the Red Sea, who had brought down the walls of Jericho, who had fed five thousand with a handful of loaves and fish, and *that* God, through the Holy Spirit, was fighting for John Mitchell.

Jessie closed her eyes and whispered one more prayer before sleep finally came: "Father, I am waiting on You. Move in John's life. Please. Move."

The next morning, she woke to a text from Pastor Mike: Prayer schedule is set, 24 people committed to one-hour shifts, John is covered in prayer around the clock, God is moving, Jessie, hold on.

She read the message three times, tears once again streaming down her face. Twenty-four people, twenty-four members of their church family who had committed to pray for John every single hour of every single day.

Downstairs, she could hear John moving around in the kitchen. She took a deep breath and went down to face another day of watching him slip further away, but this time, she was not facing it alone.

This time, she had an army; she was trusting God to do what only He could do, to reach into the darkness and pull her husband back into the light.

That evening, she went through the motions of her bedtime routine with mechanical precision. She brushed her teeth, washed her face, and changed into her pajamas. Each action felt heavy, weighted with the exhaustion of carrying fear for too long. The house was quiet now, and the kids were asleep in their rooms, their peace a stark contrast to the storm still raging in her heart.

She moved to the bedroom and sat on the edge of the bed, her phone in her hand. The screen glowed in the darkness, casting shadows across her face. Her thumb hovered over John's name in her contacts. She knew he was downstairs in the basement again. She'd heard him go down there hours ago, the door clicking shut with that same finality that had become so familiar.

With trembling fingers, she typed out a message: *John, please come to bed. I love you. We can get through this together.*

She hit send and watched the message status. One minute passed. Then two. Then five. The three dots that would indicate he was typing a reply never appeared. The message just sat there, like so many others before it.

She set the phone on the nightstand and pulled back the covers, sliding into the cold sheets. She lay on her back, staring at the ceiling, listening to the silence of the house. Sleep felt impossible. Her mind raced with images she couldn't control, his hollow eyes, the way he'd stopped smiling, the distance that had grown between them like a chasm she couldn't cross.

She closed her eyes, trying to pray, trying to find that peace she'd felt earlier at Scoops when the church family had surrounded her. But that peace felt distant now, replaced by a gnawing anxiety that would not go away.

Just go to sleep, she told herself. *Tomorrow is another day. God is moving. Pastor Mike said so. People are praying right now.*

She pulled the covers up to her chin and turned on her side, facing his empty pillow. She reached out and touched it, the fabric cool beneath her fingers. How many more nights would she sleep alone like this? How many more nights would she lie here wondering if her husband was slipping away from her, from God, from life itself?

She was just beginning to drift into an uneasy sleep when it hit her.

It came without warning, without mercy, a wave of despair so profound, so crushing, that it knocked the breath from her body. Her eyes flew open in the darkness, her heart suddenly pounding with a terror she'd never experienced before. This wasn't her normal worry, her usual fear. This was something else entirely. Something darker. Something that felt like death itself had entered the room.

Her hands began to shake. Her breath came in short, sharp gasps. Every cell in her body screamed that something was terribly, horribly wrong. It was as if a veil had been lifted, and she could truly feel the spiritual battle raging around her husband. The enemy wasn't just attacking John. He was trying to destroy him. Tonight. Right now!

"No," she whispered into the darkness, her voice breaking. "No, no, no."

Her hands fumbled for her phone on the nightstand, nearly dropping it in her panic. The screen was too bright, making her squint as she pulled up her messages. She found Rachel's name and her fingers moved with desperate speed, typing the words: *Emergency Prayers Now!*

She hit send and immediately dropped the phone on the bed. There was no time to wait for a response. No time to explain. She threw back the covers and slid out of bed, her knees hitting the hardwood floor with a thud that she barely felt.

She pressed her palms together, her whole body trembling, and began to pray. But the words wouldn't come. All that emerged was a broken sob, then another, and then the tears came in a flood she couldn't control.

"Jesus," she gasped, her voice raw with anguish. "Jesus, please."

The fear was unlike anything she'd ever known. It wrapped around her throat like hands, squeezing, suffocating. She could feel it: the darkness, the evil, the enemy's grip on her husband. It was real. It was tangible. And it was winning.

"Father God," she cried out, her voice rising in the quiet bedroom. "I'm begging You. Save him. Save John. Don't let the enemy win. Please, God, please!"

Tears streamed down her face, dripping onto her clasped hands. Her shoulders shook with the force of her sobs.

She'd been afraid before, afraid of losing John, afraid of what he might do, but this was different. This was the kind of fear that came from seeing into the spiritual realm, from understanding that this battle wasn't just emotional or mental. It was spiritual. Eternal. Life and death!

"I can't lose him," she sobbed, rocking back and forth on her knees. "God, I can't lose him. My children can't lose their father. Please, Jesus. Please intervene. Send Your angels. Surround him with Your presence. Break through the darkness. Break through!"

Her voice cracked and broke, but she kept praying, kept crying out. The words tumbled over each other, desperate, at times incoherent, but filled with a mother's love, a wife's devotion, a believer's faith that was being tested to its absolute limit.

"I bind the enemy in Jesus' name," she declared through her tears, her voice gaining strength even as her body shook. "I bind every lie, every whisper of death, every spirit of despair and hopelessness. You have no authority over John Mitchell. He belongs to God. He belongs to Jesus. You cannot have him!"

The fear didn't leave. If anything, it intensified, pressing down on her like a physical weight. But beneath it, something else began to rise, fierce determination. She would not stop praying. She would not give up. She would fight for her husband with every breath in her body, with every ounce of faith she possessed.

"God, You are stronger than the enemy," she prayed, her voice hoarse but unwavering. "You are greater than this darkness. You are the God who raises the dead, who heals the broken, who rescues the perishing. I am asking You, I am begging You, rescue John, right now, this moment, do not wait, please do not wait."

Her phone buzzed on the bed behind her, but she did not turn to look. She could not stop praying, not when she could feel the battle raging, when she could sense that this was the moment, the critical moment, when everything would either break or break through.

"Send someone to him," she pleaded, her face wet with tears. "Send our Pastor. Send a friend. Send an angel. I don't care who, just send someone. Don't let him be alone in that basement. Don't let him make a decision he can't take back. Please, God. Please."

She could go down there herself, right now. The basement was just down the hall, just a flight of stairs away. But she knew, deep in her spirit, she knew, that what John needed most in this moment was not her presence.

It was not another confrontation, another conversation, another plea. He needed God, and the most powerful thing she could do was stay right here on her knees and fight for him in prayer, so she pressed in harder, praying with everything in her.

The sobs came harder now, shaking her entire frame. She bent forward until her forehead touched the floor, her hands still clasped in prayer, her whole being crying out to heaven with a desperation that transcended words.

This was what it meant to intercede, this was what it meant to stand in the gap, this was the kind of prayer that moved mountains, that shook heaven, that refused to accept defeat.

And somewhere in the midst of her tears, in the depths of her fear, she felt it, that whisper of hope, not loud, not obvious, but there, a quiet assurance that she was not praying alone, that even now, at this very moment, others were lifting John's name to heaven, that the prayers of the righteous were powerful and effective, that God was listening.

"I trust You," she whispered, her voice barely audible. "Even though I am terrified, even though I cannot see what You are doing, I trust You. You love John more than I do. You have a plan. You are going to move. I believe it. I have to believe it."

She stayed on her knees, praying and weeping as the minutes stretched into an hour. Her knees ached, her throat was raw, her eyes burned from crying, but she did not stop, she couldn't stop.

Because somewhere in the darkness of their basement, her husband was fighting a battle he did not even know he was in, and she would pray until the battle was won, until the darkness was defeated, until God's light broke through and brought John home.

"Please, God," she whispered one more time, her voice breaking. "Please save my husband."

CHAPTER 8

WHEN HEAVEN SENT YOU

The night air was cool against John's face, carrying the usual smells of a suburban neighborhood, the smell of freshly cut grass and the smell of honeysuckle, scents that once meant comfort, but comfort now felt impossibly distant.

Behind him, the house was dark except for the bedroom window where a soft light glowed. Jessie was still awake, reading her Bible, praying for him like she did every night. If she looked out the window, she'd see him standing here. But she wouldn't know what he was holding. Wouldn't know what he was about to do.

He raised the gun slowly, his hand shaking. The metal was cold against his palm. Solid. Real. Final.

All he had to do was lift it a little higher. Three seconds, maybe four, and it would all be over. He found that he could no longer stand and fell to his knees.

"God," he whispered, his voice breaking. "Forgive me for what I'm about to do, but before I do it, please show me You are still there. Show me there is another way. I'm asking You, not as

98

someone who deserves it, but as that boy who once believed You kept Your promises."

The words felt like they were being torn from somewhere deep inside him, from that place where the seven-year-old boy who had once drawn Noah's ark with crayons still lived, buried under years of disappointment and failure. That boy had believed God could save him from anything; that boy had been so sure.

"I'm asking You now," John continued, his hands trembling. "If You are listening, if You have ever listened, answer, please answer." His voice trailed off into a whisper, one last hopeful plea for help.

The gun was back at his side, but he was lifting it, slowly, inevitably. This was it. This was the moment. In a few seconds, Jessie would hear the shot. She'd come running. She'd find him here in the weeds, and her life would shatter, but eventually, someday, she'd be okay. They'd all be okay.

His hand was shaking so badly now that he could barely hold the gun steady. The weight of it seemed to increase with each passing second, as if an invisible force was pressing down on his arm, making it nearly impossible to raise it higher. Tears streamed down his face while voices clawed at his mind, cataloging every failure, every impossible burden his life had become. His breath came in ragged gasps. The inner voices grew louder, relentless: You don't deserve to live. Your family deserves better. You lost all your savings to a scam.

"I'm sorry," he sobbed. "I'm so sorry. Jessie, Emma, Caleb, I'm sorry. I love you all. I'm so sorry."

The gun was rising. His finger was on the trigger. The moment was here.

Jessie couldn't settle.

She sat propped against the headboard, her Bible open across her lap, but the words on the page blurred together. She'd finally pulled herself up from the floor an hour ago, her knees aching, her voice hoarse from prayer. She'd tried to settle into bed, alternating between reading Scripture and crying out to God, but nothing could quiet the growing dread inside her.

Something was wrong. Something was terribly wrong. She could feel it deep inside her heart, in every instinct that screamed that John was in danger. She'd been cycling between prayer and Scripture all evening, desperately seeking peace, seeking answers, seeking anything except this suffocating fear that refused to let go.

She had watched him at dinner, barely eating, barely speaking. She'd seen the way he'd looked at the kids, really looked at them, like he was memorizing their faces. She'd felt the way he'd said "I love you" when she went to bed, like it was goodbye.

And now, lying in bed with her Bible open to Psalm 40, she couldn't shake the feeling that she was running out of time.

"Father," she prayed, her voice urgent in the quiet bedroom. "Something's wrong. I know something's wrong. Please, God, please protect John. Please don't let me lose him. Please…"

She stopped mid-prayer, her breath catching.

A warmth spread through her chest, sudden and unmistakable. Not a voice, not words, but a knowing. Clear and urgent and impossible to ignore.

Go. Now. The backyard.

Her eyes flew open. Her heart was pounding. She knew, she knew with absolute certainty, that John was in the backyard right now, and something terrible was about to happen.

She threw off the covers and ran. No shoes, no robe, just her pajamas and bare feet on the hardwood floor. Down the stairs, through the kitchen, her hand fumbling for the back door handle.

"John!" she called out, her voice breaking. "John!"

She burst through the door into the darkness, her eyes searching.

At first, she could see nothing. The backyard was a wall of black, the moon hidden behind clouds, the overgrown weeds creating layers of darkness, shadows within shadows. "Her heart hammered in her chest as she stepped outside the back door, her eyes straining into the darkness, desperate to find him."

"John!" she screamed into the darkness.

And then, slowly, her eyes began to adjust.

She saw him there, in the middle of the yard, a dark shape on the ground. At first, it looked like nothing more than a pile of discarded clothing, crumpled and lifeless among the weeds. But as her vision sharpened, she realized with horror that it was him. Her husband. Collapsed on the ground.

But there was something else.

Something that made her blood run cold.

Around him, moving in the darkness, were smaller shadows. They weren't solid; they were more like wisps of smoke, dark shapes that seemed to writhe and twist in the air around His fallen form.

They circled him with what seemed like predatory intent, pressing in closer, their movements hungry and deliberate. They were darker than the night itself, as if they absorbed the very light around them, feeding on the despair that hung thick in the air.

Jessie's breath caught in her throat. She could feel it now: the oppressive weight of evil, the tangible presence of something malevolent.

This wasn't just depression. This wasn't just despair. This was spiritual warfare, and the enemy had him surrounded.

Fear gripped her heart, squeezing like a vice. But beneath the fear, something else rose: a fierce anger.

A determination that burned hotter than her terror.

"No," she whispered. Then louder:" NO!"

She started running toward him, her bare feet pounding across the yard into the wet grass. The shadows seemed to recoil slightly at her approach, but they didn't leave. They hovered, waiting, hungry.

And then she saw it: the glint of metal in his hand.

The gun.

Time seemed to slow. She could see his arm moving, lifting the weapon with agonizing slowness. She could see his hand trembling. She could see the shadows pressing closer, whispering what she knew were lies, urging him toward death.

"JOHN, NO!" Jessie screamed.

Something supernatural surged through her body: a strength she'd never known she possessed. Her legs moved faster than they ever had. Her vision sharpened. Every muscle in her body seemed to be infused with power that wasn't her own.

She launched herself forward, her hand shooting out with impossible speed and accuracy. Her palm connected with his wrist just as he was raising the gun toward his head.

The impact sent the weapon flying from his grip. It spun through the air and landed in the thick weeds with a dull thud.

John's head snapped up, his eyes wide with shock and confusion. He looked at Jessie as if seeing a ghost, his face pale and streaked with tears.

"Jessie?" he whispered, his voice broken.

He tried to move, his hand reaching weakly toward where the gun had fallen. His movements were sluggish, defeated, like a man underwater.

"I need... I have to..." he mumbled, crawling forward on his hands and knees, searching blindly for the weapon in the darkness, but Jessie refused to let this continue as she stepped between John and the gun, planting herself firmly in his path, and when she spoke, her voice was not her own.

It seemed to echo in the backyard like the sounding of a shofar, filled with a love so fierce it could break through any darkness, but also with something else, something that came from beyond her, through her, the voice of a warrior, the voice of someone standing in the gap between life and death, between heaven and hell.

"JOHN ARON MITCHELL, STOP."

The words rang out in the darkness with such power that even the shadows seemed to shrink back.

He froze.

His hand, still reaching for the gun, stopped mid-motion. His entire body went rigid, as if an invisible force had pinned him in place. He looked up at his wife, and what he saw reflected in her face were her features and also something else, something he did not recognize, and that terrified him.

John's hands moved toward his face as if to clear away the disbelief. Light appeared to emanate from her, impossible yet undeniably supernatural, a pale blue radiance that seemed to burn through her, rippling across her skin in waves. Her eyes blazed as if a fire burned deep within her with divine purpose.

This was the power of a prayer warrior who had refused to surrender, and it paralyzed him with fear.

This wasn't an angel. John knew that. Angels were something he had never seen, spiritual beings few had ever encountered. But this? This was what happened when God answered a desperate woman's prayers and poured His power through fragile human hands. Terrible, beautiful, dangerous. His wife stood between him and forever silence, burning with a light that wasn't her own.

"You will NOT do this," she said, her voice still carrying that terrifying strength. "You will NOT give the enemy this victory. You will NOT leave your children fatherless. You will NOT abandon the calling God has on your life."

His mouth opened, but no words came out. Shame crashed over him like a wave: hot, suffocating shame that made him want to disappear into the earth. He could imagine himself through Jessie's eyes: pathetic, broken, a failure of a man who'd been about to take the coward's way out.

But beneath the shame was something else. Fear. Fear of what he saw in Jessie's face. Fear of the power that radiated from her. Fear of the truth she was speaking.

And then he heard them, something that sounded like voices, many voices, layered and indistinct, rising and falling like distant thunder rolling across the sky, a low rumble that had become a storm, gathering with terrible power and relentless purpose. People were praying, breathless and bold. Voices fierce and urgent. Voices raised, fervent and unrelenting, overlapping like thunderclaps echoing through heavy clouds, pounding against the darkness he had wrapped around himself like a worn-out cloak. God was moving. Heaven had mobilized on his behalf, and the sound of it was both terrible and beautiful, like a battle hymn sung in the heart of the storm.

The sound came from everywhere and nowhere, as supernatural as the light that seemed to be radiating from his wife.

The weight of it all hit him with such force: the shame, the fear, the disgust, the crushing realization of what he'd almost done. Great sobs of grief tore through him, shaking his entire frame.

He lay curled on his side in the weeds, his knees drawn up, his trembling hands pressed against the earth. His body convulsed with the force of his weeping, each sob ripping from somewhere deep in his chest. His hands had gone slack, fingers digging into the dirt as he wept.

"I'm sorry," he gasped between sobs, his voice broken and raw. "I'm sorry, I'm so sorry."

Her expression softened, but she didn't move from her position between John and the gun. The supernatural strength was still there, holding her upright, keeping her voice steady.

"John," she said, and now her voice was gentler, though still filled with that authority. "Look at me. Look at me!"

Slowly, painfully, he lifted his head. His face was covered in dirt and tears, his eyes red and swollen.

"You called on God to help you," she said, her voice shaking now but still strong. "You prayed for help. And He sent me. Don't you see? You, me, and God, we're here together. Right now. In this moment. You're surrounded by prayers, John. Wrapped in the intercession of everyone who loves you, who won't let you go, who are battling for your soul even as we speak. You're not alone, John. You've never been alone."

He stared at her, his mind struggling to process her words. He had prayed. Just seconds ago, he'd cried out to God for help. And now Jessie was here, standing between him and death, speaking with a voice that carried the weight of countless prayers, fueled by the love of everyone who had refused to let him go.

The shadows that had been circling him were gone now, driven back by Jessie's presence, by the authority she carried. The oppressive weight that had been crushing him began to lift, just slightly.

"How did you know?" He whispered. "How did you know I was out here?"

"I felt it," she said, and tears were streaming down her face now, though her voice remained steady," God told me. I was praying, and I just knew. I knew you were in trouble, and I knew I had to move. Right now. This second."

She took a step closer, then another, until she was kneeling beside him in the dirt and weeds. Her hand came up to his face, and her touch was warm, real, anchoring him to life.

"God heard you, John. He heard your prayer, and He sent me to find you. He sent me to fight for you. Because You're worth fighting for. Do you hear me? You're worth fighting for."

And then something changed in him. He had almost lost this battle, this war against the darkness that had nearly claimed him. He fell forward into Jessie's arms, and she caught him, holding him as he sobbed.

"I'm sorry," he gasped against her shoulder. "I'm so sorry. I was going to... I almost..."

"I know," she whispered, holding him tighter. "I know. But you didn't. You're here. You're still here."

"I don't know how to keep going," he said, his voice muffled. "I don't know how to fix this. I've destroyed everything."

"You haven't destroyed everything," she said fiercely, pulling back to look him in the eyes. "You're here. You're alive. That's what matters. Everything else, we'll figure it out together. But you have to stay, John. You have to stay with me. With us."

He looked at his wife's face in the darkness. Her cheeks were wet with tears, her hair was tangled, her pajamas were covered in dirt and grass stains. She'd run out here barefoot, in the middle of the night, because God had told her to. Because he had prayed, and God had answered.

"I prayed," he said, his voice hoarse with wonder. "I asked God for help, and He sent you."

"He did," Jessie said, smiling through her tears. "He heard you, baby. He's been hearing you all along. You just couldn't see it."

He looked past her to where the gun lay in the weeds, barely visible in the darkness. The thing that had seemed like the only solution, the only way out. Now it just looked like what it was, a tool of death, a lie disguised as mercy.

"I almost did it," he whispered. "I was seconds away."

"But you didn't," she said firmly. "You cried out to God. And He answered. He's here, John. Right here with us."

And in that moment, kneeling in the weeds with his wife's arms around him and the gun lying in the grass, he felt it. Not a voice or a vision, but a presence. Warm and solid and undeniable. The same presence he'd felt as a child in Sunday school, when faith was simple, and God's love was as real as the crayons in his hand.

God was here. God had heard him. God had sent Jessie.

"I'm so tired," he said. "I'm so tired of fighting."

"Then stop fighting," Jessie said. "Let us carry you for a while. Let God carry you. You don't have to do this alone anymore."

He nodded, unable to speak, and let her hold him. They knelt there in the overgrown backyard for a long time, holding each other in the darkness, while above them the clouds parted and moonlight spilled across the yard, illuminating the place where death had been defeated, and life had won.

Finally, she pulled back and looked at the gun lying in the weeds. "We need to get rid of that."

He nodded. "Yeah."

She picked it up carefully, her hands steady despite the trembling he could see in her shoulders. "I'm going to lock this in the car. And tomorrow, we're getting rid of it. Permanently."

"Okay."

"And we're calling Dr. Chen. Pastor Mike told me about him; he's a therapist, a Christian therapist. You're going to talk to him."

"Okay," he said again. He was too exhausted to argue, too wrung out to do anything except agree.

"And you're not sleeping in the basement anymore," she continued, her voice firm. "You're sleeping next to me, where I can see you, where I can hold you. Understood?"

"Understood."

She helped him to his feet, and they stood there for a moment, looking at each other in the moonlight. He could see the fear still lingering in her eyes, the knowledge of how close they'd come to losing everything.

"I love you," he said. "I'm sorry I put you through this. I'm sorry I..."

"Stop apologizing," she said. "Just promise me you'll stay. Promise me you'll fight. Not alone but along with me, with God, with everyone who loves you. But promise me you'll stay."

"I promise," he said, and he meant it. Because she was here, and God had sent her, and that had to mean something. That had to mean he was worth saving.

They walked back to the house together, her arm around his

waist, and he was leaning on her more than he wanted to admit. At the back door, she paused and looked at the backyard, the weeds, the darkness, the place where he had almost ended his life.

"We're going to fix that," she said. "We're going to clean it up, plant a garden, and make it beautiful. A reminder that God can bring life out of darkness."

He nodded, too tired to speak.

Inside, she locked the gun in the car, then led him upstairs to their bedroom. She helped him out of his coat, his father's old work jacket, heavy with the weight of what he'd almost done. After brief showers to wash away the dirt, grass, and adrenaline, she guided him to the bed.

"Lie down," she said gently.

He lay down, and she climbed in beside him, pulling him close. Her arms wrapped around him, holding him like she was afraid he might disappear if she let go.

"I'm not going anywhere," he whispered.

"I know," she said. "But I'm holding you anyway."

They lay there in the darkness, his head on her chest, her hand stroking his hair. He could hear her heartbeat, steady and strong, and feel the rise and fall of her breathing. She was real. She was here. God had sent her.

"Jessie?" He said after a long silence.

"Yeah?"

"How did you know? Really. How did you know to come to the backyard right at that moment?"

She was quiet for a moment. "I was praying and reading Psalm 40. And I got to the part about God hearing our cry and drawing us up from the pit. And suddenly, I just knew. It wasn't a voice, exactly. It was more like... a knowing. A certainty. Like God was saying, "Go now. Right now. He needs you." She paused. "So I ran. I didn't even think about it. I just ran."

"What if you hadn't?" He asked. "What if you'd ignored it, or thought it was just your imagination?"

"But I didn't," she said firmly. "God made sure I didn't. He made sure I heard Him, and He made sure I listened. Because He loves you, John. He's not done with you yet."

He closed his eyes, tears leaking out again. "I don't deserve that kind of love."

"None of us do," she said. "That's what makes it grace."

They fell silent again, holding each other in the darkness. Outside, the night continued: stars wheeling, wind rustling through the trees, the world turning on its axis.

But inside this room, time seemed to stand still. A moment of grace, of rescue, of two prayers colliding in the darkness.

He had cried out to God for help.

And God had sent Jessie.

And somehow, impossibly, miraculously, he was still here. Still breathing. Still alive.

One battle won, but the war raged on. Unemployment, fore-closure, depression - enemy forces still massing on the horizon. Tomorrow would demand new strategies, new strength. But tonight belonged to them. Tonight, they'd held the line, and that was everything.

Tonight, he was alive. And she was holding him. And God had shown up in the weeds and the darkness and the absolute lowest moment of his life.

That had to be enough. For tonight, that had to be enough.

"Thank you," he whispered, not sure if he was talking to Jessie or to God or to both.

"You're welcome," she whispered back. "Now sleep. I've got you. I'm not letting go."

And for the first time in months, he believed her.

He closed his eyes and let himself drift, held by his wife's arms and God's grace, knowing that when morning came, he'd still be here. Still broken, still struggling, but still alive.

Still here.

CHAPTER 9
ARMOR FOR WAR

L ight.

That was the first thing he noticed when he opened his eyes. Everything felt different. The gray, filtered light that had become his constant companion over the past few months was gone, and in its place, soft golden light streamed through the bedroom window in thick beams that seemed almost solid enough to touch.

He blinked, disoriented. For a moment, he couldn't remember where he was or why his body ached as if he'd been in a fight. Then it all came rushing back: the backyard, the gun, the shadows, Jessie's voice cutting through the darkness like a sword.

You called on God to help you, and He sent me.

He turned his head on the pillow and found her watching him from the chair beside the bed. Fresh clothes. That ponytail he loved. Eyes heavy with exhaustion. And still, the tenderness in her expression, the relief and love radiating from her face, made his heart swell until he thought it might burst from the sheer joy of being loved by this woman.

A soft smile crossed her face when their eyes met, the kind of smile that came from knowing someone completely, from having weathered storms together. She rose from the chair and moved to sit on the edge of the bed.

"How do you feel?" she asked, her voice gentle but steady. His voice was hoarse, from the battle in the night as he considered the question.

How did he feel? His body was sore, his eyes felt swollen, and his head ached. But beneath all that, there was something else. Something he hadn't felt in so long he'd almost forgotten what it was.

Hope. A quiet, steady hope that whispered, You are still here, you made it through the night, you are not alone.

He did feel different this morning: lighter, better, stronger. He could still see it, last night kneeling beside the bed in the dark, Jessie's hand warm in his.

He had started, his voice rough. "I've been so angry. At you. At myself. And I've used that anger like a wall, and I'm sorry." The words had felt dangerous coming out, like admitting defeat, but she squeezed his hand tighter, showing him it was okay and to keep going.

They had stayed there, kneeling, their prayers tangling together, asking for forgiveness, for strength, for the ability to love each other through whatever came next, not the polished prayers of Sunday mornings but the kind that came from somewhere deeper, from a place where only God could go.

When she finally whispered, "Amen," he felt something change. The knot he had been carrying in his chest for months, since the layoff and since the silence had started, loosened just slightly, just enough.

He had fallen asleep feeling better than he had in years, truly at peace.

Now, as he thought more about how he felt, he said.

"Different," he said finally, "I feel different."

She reached down and took his hand, threading her fingers through his. "You look different, too, the light." She paused, searching for words. "It is like you can actually see it now, like it's reaching you."

He looked toward the window again. She was right. The light did seem brighter, more vivid. Or maybe it was just that he was actually seeing it as it always had been, instead of just existing in the gray fog that had become his world.

"What time is it?" he asked.

"Almost nine. I let you sleep. You needed it."

Nine o'clock. On a weekday. The kids would be at school. Jessie should be at work. But here she was, sitting beside him, keeping watch.

"You called in?" He asked.

"I did. Told them I had a family emergency." Her voice was matter-of-fact, but he could hear the tremor beneath it. "Which is true."

He sat up slowly, every muscle protesting. He looked down at his hands, clean yet haunted by memories of dirt under his fingernails and grass stains on his palms, remnants of how close he'd come.

"I can't believe I almost...," he started, his voice wavering.

Jessie leaned in, her eyes filled with compassion. "You're here now, and that is what matters."

He shook his head, "I feel like I failed everyone."

"No, you didn't fail. You're fighting a war, and that takes strength," she said gently. "You're not alone in this; we can figure this out together."

He nodded, not trusting himself to speak. The memories were still so fresh, so raw. The weight of the gun in his hand. The cold metal against his palm. The absolute certainty that it was the only way out.

And then Jessie, appearing like an angel in the darkness, knocked the gun away with impossible strength, standing between him and death. He blinked, pulling himself back from the memory, back to this room, to safety, to her watching over him. The rich aroma of coffee drifted through the air. " I smell coffee," he said, grasping at the normalcy of it before the emotions could overwhelm him again.

She smiled. "I made a pot. Thought we could both use it. Come on, let's go downstairs."

She helped him out of bed, and he was grateful for her steadying hand. His legs felt weak, shaky, like he'd been sick for a long time and was just now trying to walk again. In a way, he supposed, that was exactly what had happened.

They made their way downstairs together, her arm around his waist. The house was quiet. No kids arguing over the bathroom, no morning cartoons blaring from the TV. Just the two of them and the sunlight streaming through every window.

In the kitchen, she poured two mugs of coffee and handed one to him. He wrapped both hands around it, feeling the warmth seep into his palms, and took a sip. It was strong and hot and exactly what he needed.

For a moment, they just stood there in the kitchen, drinking their coffee in silence. He looked around at the familiar space: the chipped countertop, the fridge covered in the kids' artwork, the calendar on the wall with all of Jessie's shifts marked in red. This was his life. This was what he'd almost left behind.

"I'm sorry," he said quietly. "For everything. For putting you through this. For..."

She reached out, touching his arm, not to stop him but to steady him. "John," she said softly, "We'll talk through all of this, every part of it, and we will. But right now, I just need you here with me, just for this moment. Can you do that?"

He nodded. "Yeah. I can do that."

He took another sip of coffee, savoring the bitter warmth. The light coming through the kitchen window caught the steam rising from his mug, turning it into something almost ethereal. Everything seemed sharper this morning, more vivid. The colors brighter, the sounds clearer. Like he'd been living underwater and had finally broken the surface.

"The kids," he said suddenly. "Do they know?"

"No," she said firmly. "And they don't need to. Not yet. Not like this. When the time is right, when you're ready, we'll figure out what to tell them. But for now, they just know Daddy wasn't feeling well, and Mommy stayed home to take care of him."

He felt a wave of relief wash over him. He couldn't face Emma and Caleb right now, couldn't look into their innocent faces knowing what he'd almost done. Not yet.

"Thank you," he said.

They stood in comfortable silence for a few more minutes, drinking their coffee and watching the morning light play across the kitchen floor. He felt something release in his spirit, like a fist that had been clenched for months finally beginning to open. The crushing weight that had been pressing down on him started to lift, slowly. Not gone, but lighter. Bearable.

And then there was a knock at the door.

Jessie's eyes met his, and he saw something there: not quite guilt, but close to it.

"Who is that?" He asked, though part of him already knew.

"It's Pastor Mike," she said quietly," I called him this morning. I asked him to come."

He felt uneasy. Pastor Mike. The man who'd known him since he was a kid, who'd married him and Jessie, who'd baptized both their children, the man who represented everything he had been running from: church, faith, community, accountability.

"Jessie, no," he said, taking a step back. "I can't. I'm not ready."

"John," she said, her voice gentle but firm. "We need help. Real help. And he can connect us with resources, with people who can actually help us get through this."

The knock came again, more insistent this time.

He looked at her, and what he saw in her face stopped his

protest. She wasn't asking. This was happening whether he was ready or not. And beneath his panic, beneath his shame, he knew she was right. He couldn't do this alone. He'd tried that, and it had nearly killed him.

"I don't want him to know," he said, his voice barely above a whisper. "I don't want him to see me like this."

The words hung in the air, and suddenly he could hear the childlike whine in that whisper. He cringed inwardly. Here he was, trying to hide from the pastor because he didn't want him to know how badly he had failed his family and his God.

"He already knows you're struggling," she said. "Everyone has been praying, John. We've been praying for you. This isn't a surprise. He's here because he cares about you, about us, about our family."

Another knock, followed by Pastor Mike's voice. "Jessie? John? It's Mike. Can I come in?"

He closed his eyes, feeling the shame wash over him in waves. Hot, suffocating shame that made him want to run, to hide, to disappear. The pastor was going to find out what he'd almost done. What kind of man he'd become. What a failure he was.

But then another thought cut through the shame: *If I'd been successful last night, this would be a very different visit from the pastor.*

He opened his eyes and looked at Jessie. She was watching him with such love, such fierce determination, that he immediately forgot about the feelings of shame. She'd saved his life last night. She'd run into the darkness and fought for him when he couldn't fight for himself. The least he could do was trust her now.

"Okay," he said quietly. "Okay."

Jessie squeezed his hand, then went to answer the door. He heard the front door open, heard Mike's warm voice greeting her, heard their footsteps coming toward the kitchen.

He set his coffee mug down on the counter and turned to face the doorway, his heart pounding. He wanted to run. He wanted to hide. He wanted to be anywhere but here, about to face the man who'd known him most of his life and see the disappointment in his eyes.

But he stayed. Because Jessie had asked him to. Because he'd promised her he would stay, would fight, would let people help him.

He appeared in the doorway, and he braced himself for judgment, for disappointment, for the look that said, I expected better from you.

But that's not what he saw.

Pastor Mike's face was full of compassion, yes, but also something else, relief, deep, profound relief, like he'd been holding his breath for months and could finally exhale.

"John," Mike said, his voice thick with emotion. "Thank God. Thank God you're here."

And then, to his complete shock, Mike crossed the kitchen in three quick strides and pulled him into a tight hug.

He stood there, frozen, his arms at his sides. He couldn't remember the last time another man had hugged him like this, with such genuine affection, such relief, such lack of judgment.

"I'm so glad you're okay," he said, his voice muffled against his shoulder. "We've been so worried about you."

The walls he had built over weeks of isolation crumbled in that moment under the simple, steady pressure of being seen, being known, being loved anyway. He felt his arms come up slowly, awkwardly, to return the embrace. " I'm sorry," John said, his voice cracking. "I'm so sorry."

After a moment, Mike stepped back, giving John space but keeping his eyes steady on him.

"No," Mike said, his voice softening as he held his gaze. "Not apologies, not right now. I know you're carrying shame and guilt. That is normal. But listen to me: that's not what God sees when He looks at you. He sees someone He's already forgiven. Already claimed." He paused. "Romans 8:1 says, 'There is now no condemnation for those who are in Christ Jesus.' You're here. You're alive. And more than that, you're His."

He paused again, his voice steady. "You see, John, forgiveness is part of the plan. Part of God's plan. What we need to do is to be sure that you have prayed for that forgiveness, received an answer, and understand that what you tried to do was wrong."

He looked at the pastor's face, really looked at it, and saw no judgment there. No disappointment. Just love and concern and relief.

"Jessie told me what happened last night," he said gently. "Not all the details, but enough. John, I want you to know that what you're going through, what you've been feeling, doesn't make you weak. It doesn't make you less of a man."

John felt a lump rise in his throat. "I almost..." His voice drifted off, unable to continue.

Mike shifted in his chair, his demeanor calm. "What matters is you're here now. You chose to stay, and that shows courage."

Jessie appeared with a mug of coffee, setting it down on the table in front of Mike. They settled into chairs around the table.

Mike leaned forward, his voice taking on a more serious tone. "But I need you to understand something, John. What happened last night wasn't just a bad moment. It wasn't just depression or circumstance; it was all of those things, but it was also an attack. You were under siege."

John looked up, confused. "Attack?"

"Spiritual attack," Mike said firmly. "The enemy does not want you here. He does not want your family intact. He does not want your marriage restored or your faith rebuilt. Scripture tells us in John 10:10 that the thief comes to steal, kill, and destroy. Last night, he came for you. You see, John, God has a plan, not just for you, but for every one of His children, and that is what you are. God has a purpose for you, and the enemy does not want you to realize that plan."

"Now, John I know a lot of this may feel difficult or even feel overwhelming but I'm here to help and to provide support".

"For we wrestle not against flesh and blood," Mike continued, "but against principalities, against powers, against the rulers of darkness of this world. Ephesians 6:12. This is spiritual warfare, John, and you've been fighting this battle in your own strength. That's a battle you can't win without preparation, belief, prayer, and faith."

Jessie reached across the table and took John's hand. Mike noticed and nodded.

"I don't want to overload you with Bible verses," Mike said, "but I also know that the word of God is the most powerful weapon in your arsenal. I don't want this to feel like a sermon. If you have a question or don't understand, just let me know. I have all of the scriptures we're going to go over in some paperwork so you can go back and study them later."

"I think that is very important in overcoming great difficulties like these problems you have been facing."

He leaned forward, his voice taking on a gentle but firm urgency. "What you need, John, is the full Armor of God. Scripture tells us, "Wherefore take unto you the whole armour of God, that ye may be able to withstand in the evil day, and having done all, to stand."

Mike held up his hand, counting off each piece on his fingers. "Stand therefore, having your loins girt about with truth. And having on the breastplate of righteousness.

He continued, "And your feet shod with the preparation of the gospel of peace. You need to be ready, grounded in the peace that only He can give. Above all, taking the shield of faith, wherewith ye shall be able to quench all the fiery darts of the wicked."

Mike's eyes locked with John's. "Those darts are coming at you right now, doubt, fear, but faith is your shield. And take the helmet of salvation and the sword of the Spirit, which is the word of God."

He paused, letting the words settle. "This isn't just poetry, John, though it sure is beautiful. This is your battle plan."

"But here's the truth that the enemy doesn't want you to know," the pastor said, his eyes intense. "Greater is He that is in you than he that is in the world. Last night, John, when you were at your lowest point, when the enemy had you convinced there was no way out, you cried out to God. In that moment of surrender, when you admitted you couldn't fight this alone, you did the most powerful thing a man can do. You called on the name of the Lord. And God met you right there in that moment of desperation."

"I don't feel very powerful," John said quietly.

"That's because real power in the Kingdom of God doesn't look like what the world tells you it should," Mike replied. "Real power is found in humility. In reliance on God. In prayer. Jesus Himself spent entire nights in prayer before facing His battles. If the Son of God needed prayer, how much more do we?"

Mike stood and walked to the window, looking out before turning back to face them both.

"This family has been under siege, and I don't think either of you fully recognized it until now. The arguments, the distance, the despair. Those weren't just happening to you. They were strategic. Calculated. The enemy studies us, finds our weak points, and exploits them. But John, Jessie," he looked at both of them now, "God didn't bring you through last night just to leave you defenseless. He's showing you that this battle requires different weapons."

"What do you mean?" Jessie asked.

"I mean that the weapons of our warfare are not carnal, but mighty through God to the pulling down of strongholds," Mike said. "Prayer isn't just something we do before meals or at bedtime. Prayer is our direct line to the Commander of Heaven's armies. It's how we access power that's not our own. It's how we invite God into the trenches with us."

He moved back to the table and sat down. "John, I want you to start praying again. Not just rote prayers or religious words. I mean real, honest, desperate prayer. The kind you prayed last night. The kind where you hold nothing back from God."

"I don't even know how anymore," John admitted. "I feel like... like I'm not worthy to even ask Him for anything after everything I've done."

"And that's exactly what the enemy wants you to believe," Mike said, his voice more passionate now. "He wants you paralyzed by shame. But God's not standing far off waiting for you to clean yourself up, John. He's right here, ready to fight for you. The moment you call on His name, you access power that makes the darkness tremble."

Mike pulled out his worn Bible from his jacket pocket and flipped through pages marked with decades of use. "Listen to this. James 4:7. "Submit yourselves therefore to God. Resist the devil, and he will flee from you." "Flee, John. Not stick around. Not keep harassing you. He flees. But notice the order. First submission to God, then resistance to the enemy. You can't fight this battle without being connected to the Source of all power."

"That small thing is what a lot of people miss when they are fighting battles. They read that scripture, "Resist the devil, and he will flee from you. But they miss the first part, the most important part: submission. And that is the critical part."

The three of them in the kitchen, the morning light streaming through the windows, the smell of coffee in the air. John felt like he was seeing everything through new eyes: the concern on Mike's face, the love in Jessie's eyes, the simple fact that he was still here to see any of it.

"I don't know how to come back from this," he said quietly. "I don't know how to fix what's broken."

"You don't have to fix it alone," Mike said. "That's why I'm here. That's why Jessie called me. We're going to walk through this together. But more than that, we're going to fight together.

Starting right now, we're going to cover this home, this marriage, this family in prayer. We're going to build a hedge of protection that the enemy can't penetrate."

The pastor stood. "In fact, before we pray, there are a few things I need to go over with you. Because faith isn't passive, John. Faith is active. It's a choice to believe that God is who He says He is, even when everything in your circumstances screams otherwise. And the enemy needs to know that this family is no longer undefended territory."

Jessie stood as well, still holding John's hand. John felt rooted to his chair, overwhelmed.

"I want you both to know," Mike continued, "that this isn't going to be easy. The enemy doesn't give up territory without a fight. But when God's people stand together, when they pray in agreement, when they choose faith over fear, that's when we see breakthrough. That's when strongholds crumble. That's when marriages are restored, and families are healed."

He extended his hand toward John. "So will you let us fight with you, John? Will you let us stand in the gap until you're strong enough to stand on your own? Will you choose faith, even if it's just a mustard seed's worth right now?"

John looked at the hand extended toward him, then at Jessie's tear-filled eyes, then back at Mike's steady gaze. Slowly, he stood and took the pastor's hand.

"I'm ready," John said, his voice stronger than before. "I'm ready to fight back. Mike nodded, his grip firm and reassuring. "That's what I needed to hear. And you won't be doing this alone." He released John's hand and reached into his bag, pulling out some printed materials. "I brought some resources with me. Information about counseling, support groups, and some Scripture guides for spiritual warfare. But before we go through all of this, let's sit down."

He gestured toward the kitchen table. "I want to hear more about how you feel. How are you really doing?"

He looked at Jessie, who nodded encouragingly. Then he looked back at Mike, at this man who'd known him most of his life, yet was still here, still showing up, still refusing to give up on him.

"I'm scared," he admitted. "I'm ashamed. I'm exhausted. But I'm here. And that's more than I thought I'd be able to say this morning."

"That's enough," Mike said. "For right now, that's more than enough."

They moved back to the kitchen table, and Jessie poured Mike another cup of coffee. As they sat down together, he felt something he hadn't felt in months: not hope exactly, but the possibility of hope. The sense that maybe, just maybe, there was a way forward.

The light continued to stream through the windows, bright, warm, and real. He let himself believe that hope wasn't just an illusion.

John was quiet for a moment, then looked down at his hands, his voice barely above a whisper. "I can't help but think about what I've been through, what I'm still going through. Before all this started, before the plant closed down, I really thought I was a solid Christian. I attended church regularly, but I have to admit I wasn't nearly as good a Christian as I thought I was. I can see now that I really wasn't getting the job done with praying or reading the Bible, and that seems like a big part of what caused me to..."

His voice trailed off into silence. Mike leaned forward again.

"The church is facing a serious crisis. There are a lot of people who attend church, and even though they are good people, they are not all saved. What is really concerning is that in many instances, they are unaware of their eternal condition.

"But with prayer, you can ask for help to understand better. We need to be in constant prayer, building that foundation before the trials come. That's how we prepare ourselves to face the weaknesses of our human condition."

That is what Paul meant in Philippians 2:12: "Wherefore, my beloved, as ye have always obeyed, not as in my presence only, but now much more in my absence, work out your own salvation with fear and trembling." "What Paul was saying is that we have to be careful to stay close to the Lord, because our human condition can be quickly deceived. We can fool ourselves into thinking we are fantastic Christians when the real truth may not be what we thought it was."

Mike paused. "Now, I don't want to overload you. Is this too much?"

He shook his head. "No, it makes sense. I was praying the same prayer over and over again, only it wasn't really a prayer, not like how Jessie prays. I knew it too, but I also didn't realize how much I didn't know about reading the Bible and praying."

"This is good," continued the pastor," we have covered some Bible here, and there is more bible reading here in these papers. But also, I want to share some other subjects. I have some information in case you need additional resources. There are Christian therapists and even medication, if it is necessary and appropriate. Sometimes depression can be overwhelming and severely disruptive. I want you to know that there are many different resources to help you and your family, and we are here for you as a community and a church."

John nodded again.

"I want to leave you with this," Mike said. "Hebrews 4:12: 'For the word of God is quick, and powerful, and sharper than any twoedged sword, piercing even to the dividing asunder of soul and spirit, and of the joints and marrow, and is a discerner of the thoughts and intents of the heart.' That is a powerful Scripture, but most importantly, you need to get into the habit of reading the Word, all of your family together. Make it a daily thing. You will never regret doing that, and it will help you in ways that you might not expect."

"Let's pray."

Mike lowered his head and began. "Thank you, Heavenly Father, for this miracle. This was a spiritual battle that, without Your help, would have had a very different outcome. We thank You for what You have done here, and we ask that You keep this family in Your care. Keep them safe. Help them overcome this battle and come out on the other side stronger than before. We thank You for everything You have done and for what You will do in the future. Amen."

Mike stood and hugged John again. "If you need me, call. Day or night, and I mean that. I'll see you in a few days, or if you need me, call sooner."

He stepped back, his expression serious but filled with care. "Be sure to study those Bible guides together, and look at the family study guide for praying and reading the Bible as a family. It is so very important for your children's future and the spiritual health of your family as a whole." He paused, letting the weight of his words settle. "This is one of the hardest things for a family to maintain, but it is also the single most powerful thing you can do as a family."

John thanked the pastor. Jessie followed him to the door and thanked him as well, then closed the door and locked it.

They stood there for a moment. He said, "I learned a lot today."

Jessie nodded. "I did too."

"Will you teach me how to read the Bible and, more importantly, how to understand it?"

Jessie looked at him with tender honesty. "Yes, though I don't understand it all myself. I'm not an expert, John. There's so much I don't know, so much I'm still learning."

"That's fine," he said quietly. "Maybe we can learn together."

Her eyes brightened. "I'd like that. I really would. We can study together, ask Pastor Mike questions when we are unsure."

He paused, gathering his courage. "I also want to learn to pray like you do."

She shook her head gently, a soft smile on her face. "That will come. The more you read, the better you get at praying. But honestly, I don't think I'm that great at it either. I just talk to God like I would talk to anyone I love. Sometimes I stumble over my words, sometimes I don't know what to say at all."

"But you knew what to say last night," John said.

"Last night I was desperate," she admitted. "And sometimes that's when the most honest prayers come out. But John, we can learn this together. Both of us. We can grow in this together. I don't want you thinking I've got it all figured out, because I don't. But maybe that's okay. Maybe we're supposed to figure it out as a team."

He squeezed her hand.

Outside, morning light poured through the windows, spreading golden beams across the room and settling over them with a steady love and a quiet, fragile hope that anything was still possible.

CHAPTER 10

THE DARK PLACE

Three days.

And already, John felt himself sinking. Pastor Mike's words about faith being active, about this being a battle had sounded so clear, so possible in the moment. But now, alone with his thoughts and the weight of everything still broken, it felt overwhelming. Three days, and already he was learning that healing wasn't a straight line.

But this morning, driving his truck through the quiet streets of their neighborhood, he felt something he hadn't felt in a long time: useful. Productive. Like maybe he still had something to offer the world.

Mrs. Henderson had called yesterday, her voice trembling with that particular anxiety of the elderly facing a household emergency. Her water heater had given out, completely dead, with water pooling on her basement floor. She'd heard through the church prayer chain that John was good with his hands, that he'd worked maintenance at the factory for years before the closure.

"I know you're going through a hard time, dear," she'd said. "But I didn't know who else to call. Those plumbers want to charge me an arm and a leg, and I don't want to burden my son with every problem I face."

He had surprised himself by saying yes. Not because he needed the money, though God knew he did, but because it felt good to be needed. To have someone believe he could fix something.

Now, pulling into Mrs. Henderson's driveway, he grabbed his toolbox from the truck bed and headed to the basement door. The work had taken most of the morning: disconnecting the old water heater, hauling it up the basement stairs, installing the new one, running new copper lines to replace the corroded ones, and then tackling the kitchen faucet that had been dripping for months.

It was good, honest work. The kind that made his hands ache and his mind quiet. The kind where you could see the results of your labor immediately: water flowing clear and hot, no leaks, everything functioning the way it should.

Mrs. Henderson had hovered nearby for most of it, bringing him lemonade and cookies, chattering about her grandchildren and the church potluck next week. She didn't ask about the factory, didn't mention his absence from Sunday services, didn't probe into the" hard time" she'd alluded to on the phone. She just treated him like John the handyman, John who could fix things, John who was helpful and competent and needed.

It was a gift, though she probably didn't realize how important it was for him to feel needed.

By early afternoon, he was tightening the last connection on the kitchen faucet, testing the hot and cold water, making sure everything was secure. Mrs. Henderson stood beside him, her weathered hands clasped together, watching the water flow with the kind of joy that only comes from having gone without something essential and finally having it restored; that was something John could understand.

"Oh, John," she said, her eyes tearing up. "It's perfect. Just perfect. I can't thank you enough."

He wiped his hands on a rag and started packing up his tools. "It's not a big deal, Mrs. Henderson. Just basic plumbing."

"It's a very big deal to me," she insisted. Then, reaching for her purse on the counter, she asked the question he'd been dreading. "How much do I owe you?"

He did a quick mental calculation. He'd been there since eight that morning, and it was now almost two. Six hours of work, give or take. The factory had paid him thirty-two dollars an hour, but that was with benefits and union protections. For a simple handyman job, for a widow probably on a fixed income, for someone from the church...

"One twenty-five," he said, the number coming out before he'd fully thought it through.

Mrs. Henderson's eyebrows rose. "That's all? John, that seems too low. You've been here all day."

"It's fair," he said firmly. "Really. It's what I'd charge anyone."

It wasn't, of course. He'd probably undercharged by half. But seeing the relief on Mrs. Henderson's face as she counted out the bills from her worn wallet made it worth it.

She pressed the money into his hand, then covered his hand with both of hers. "You're a good man, John Mitchell. Don't let anyone tell you different."

He felt his throat tighten. If she only knew. If she knew what he'd almost done three nights ago, would she still think he was a good man?

But he just smiled and thanked her, gathered his tools, and headed back to his truck.

Sitting in the driver's seat, he counted the bills again. One hundred and twenty-five dollars. It wasn't much. It wouldn't even make a dent in what they owed. But it was something. Something he'd earned with his own hands, his own skills. Something that proved he wasn't completely useless.

He started the truck and headed home, and for the first time in what felt like forever, he felt something close to pride. The earned kind, the kind that came from honest work, from helping someone, from being useful again. Maybe this was how it started, he thought. Maybe this was how you crawled out of the pit: one small job at a time, one day at a time, one moment of feeling like yourself again.

The drive home took fifteen minutes, and he spent it mentally calculating. If he could get a few more jobs like this, if word spread through the church that he was available for handyman work, maybe he could cobble together enough to keep them afloat until he found something more permanent. It wasn't the factory salary, but it was something. It was a start.

He pulled into the driveway, grabbed his toolbox, and headed for the front door. Jessie wouldn't be home for another few hours. She was still at work, and the kids were still at school. The house was quiet, peaceful. He set his toolbox by the door and walked to the mailbox at the end of the driveway. Bills, probably. Junk mail. Maybe another rejection letter from a job application. He'd learned to brace himself for those. But for a moment, he paused at the end of the driveway, mail in hand, and looked around.

The neighborhood was quiet, trees swaying gently in the breeze, new green grass catching the afternoon light. It was the kind of ordinary beauty he'd stopped noticing somewhere along the way. He took a breath, then turned and walked back into the house.

He flipped through the stack as he stood in the kitchen. Electric bill. Credit card statement. Grocery store flyer. His hand froze on a pink envelope. Pink. The color of trouble. The color bill collectors used when they were done being polite, when they wanted you to know they weren't playing around anymore.

A bright pink envelope, impossible to miss among the white and manila. And on the front, in bold red letters that seemed to scream at him:

FORECLOSURE NOTICE – IMPORTANT LEGAL DOCUMENTS ENCLOSED

He couldn't move, couldn't make his feet take another step. He stared at the envelope in his hands, at those red letters that seemed to pulse and throb, growing larger with each heartbeat. This wasn't happening. It couldn't be. Not today, not after feeling hope and the joy of being useful again.

His hands were shaking as he tore open the envelope. The words blurred as he read. The page was dense with legal language, but certain phrases leapt out at him, each one landing like a blow:

...failure to make mortgage payments...

...initiation of foreclosure proceedings...

...strongly advised to consult with an attorney...

...thirty (30) days to respond...

The floor seemed to move under his feet. He felt his knees buckle, and suddenly he was on the kitchen floor, the letter falling from his hands, the other mail scattering around him. The pink envelope lay face up on the tile, those red letters still screaming: FORECLOSURE!

It felt like being hit. Not metaphorically, actually hit. Like someone had punched him in the chest and knocked all the air from his lungs. His vision tunneled, darkness creeping in at the edges. His heart was racing, pounding so hard he could hear it in his ears.

This was the thing he'd been dreading, the inevitable consequence of months of unemployment.

They were going to lose the house. Emma and Caleb were going to lose their home, their rooms, their sense of security. Jessie was going to lose the house she'd made into a home, the place where they'd brought both babies from the hospital, where they'd celebrated birthdays and Christmases and ordinary Tuesday nights.

And it was his fault. All his fault.

He felt it then, that familiar darkness, that crushing weight pressing down on him, the same feeling he'd had in the backyard three nights ago when the gun had felt like the only solution, that sense of being utterly helpless, completely overwhelmed, drowning in circumstances he couldn't control.

The shadows were back. He could feel them closing in, whispering their lies, telling him he'd failed again, that he'd never be able to fix this, that his family would be better off without him.

You're worthless. You can't provide for them. You're going to lose everything. They would be better off if you were gone, the life insurance would pay off the house...

His breath came in short, sharp gasps. His chest felt tight, constricted. The kitchen floor was cold and hard beneath him, but he couldn't seem to move, couldn't seem to do anything except stare at that pink envelope and feel the weight of his failure crashing in on him.

And then, something else surfaced. Not a thought at first more like a feeling, a warmth spreading through the cold panic. The sensation of other hands, weathered and papery-soft, covering his own. The smell of lavender and old books. A voice, gentle but firm, cutting through the panic in his head. *"You're a good man, John Mitchell. Don't let anyone tell you different."* Mrs. Henderson. The memory crystallized, became solid, real as the floor beneath his him. Her kitchen. Her hands. Her words.

Three hours ago, he had believed her. Three hours ago, he had felt it in his heart: he was useful, he was capable, he was good. And then the arrival of a pink envelope had tried to convince him otherwise, had tried to drag him back into the lie that he was worthless, that his family would be better off without him.

But he had just proven he was not worthless. He had fixed a water heater, he had helped an elderly woman, he had earned money with his own hands.

That was real. That was true. And no foreclosure notice, no matter how pink, no matter how loudly those red letters screamed, could erase that.

The frustration rose then, sharp and sudden, not at himself but at the darkness trying to convince him that one bad moment in a good day could undo the truth he'd just lived, at the lies that kept circling back, refusing to accept defeat. "Enough." The word left his mouth like a command.

He pushed himself to his feet, standing straighter, fists clenched, his hands trembling as he spoke. "You've had your time. You've said your piece. Now it's my turn."

His voice shook as he spoke, but there was steel in it. "I am not yours. I never was. Submit yourselves therefore to God. Resist the devil, and he will flee from you. I submit myself to God right here, right now!"

The words hung in the kitchen air. The darkness seemed to sense it too, a shift in the battlefield, but John's defiance lasted only a moment, the frustration draining from him as quickly as it had come, replaced by something deeper.

He sank to his knees in surrender to something greater, his eyes closing as tears streamed down his face, but his jaw remained set like stone as he began to pray. "God," he whispered, his voice shaking, "Help me. Please. I need Your help to win this battle. I cannot do this by myself." "I submit myself to You Lord!"

The words came out halting, broken. But he kept going.

"I'm scared. I'm so scared. We're going to lose this house. I don't know how to fix this. I don't know what to do."

He felt a warmth spreading through his chest, starting small and then growing, expanding, pushing back against the darkness. It wasn't dramatic. There was no voice from heaven, no vision, no angelic visitation. But it was real. Undeniably, unmistakably real.

God was here.

Not just listening from some distant heaven, but here. In this kitchen. With him on the floor, surrounded by scattered mail and the pink envelope that screamed FORECLOSURE.

His eyes opened, and he stared at his arms in amazement. The hairs were standing straight up, and he could feel it, actually feel it, like electricity in the air, like the moment before a thunderstorm when everything is charged and alive. This was real not imagination.

"You're here," he whispered, his voice filled with wonder. "You're actually here."

The warmth in his heart grew stronger. The darkness that had been pressing in began to retreat, not all at once, but steadily, surely.

The whispers of the shadows grew fainter, drowned out by something else, not a voice, but a knowing. A certainty.

You are not alone. You have never been alone. I am with you.

His voice shook as he spoke, but there was steel in it. "I am not yours. I never was. Submit yourselves therefore to God, resist the devil, and he will flee from you. I submit myself to God right here, right now!"

His prayer changed. The words came faster now, stronger, more confident. Everything was different, the foreclosure notice was still lying on the floor, the thirty-day deadline still ticking, but now something inside him had changed.

Words continued to rise from deep within, genuine and unguarded. Give me the wisdom to recognize the next right step and the courage to take it, even when the way ahead feels unclear. Give me provision, and also help me with the patience that waiting requires, help me with the strength to be the husband Jessie relies on and the father my children look up to.

Help me with grace to face my own failures and humility to accept help when it comes. Grant me faith that You're still at work, even when everything feels quiet.

"I'm not going back to the darkness," he said, his voice growing firmer. "I'm not going back to that dark place. I'm not going to the backyard. I'm not going back to believing the lies."

He pushed himself up to his knees, his hands pressed firmly against the cold tile floor. The presence he felt earlier was still there, still real, still undeniable.

He straightened. The whispers that had followed him for months, the accusations, the despair, the constant weight were just noise, empty noise. Jesus was in charge, not fear, not the voice that told him he was finished.

Jesus finished it. He won. That was the truth that flooded John's heart now, washing away the darkness. The last words of Jesus on the cross echoed in his mind: "It is finished." And it was finished, the sin debt had been paid, the victory already won. John was free of the darkness that had held him captive, free because Jesus had finished it, finished the work of grace on the cross.

The truth wasn't just something John knew anymore, it was something he felt, something that filled the hollow places fear had carved out. Christ's power wasn't distant, because it was here now, in his heart and his soul.

"I am Free of this Darkness!"

The words rang out in the kitchen with a power that surprised him. This wasn't the broken, defeated John who'd stood in the darkness three nights ago. This wasn't the hollow shell of a man who'd gone through the motions of prayer while feeling nothing. This was different.

This was a man who'd been to the edge of death and come back. A man who'd felt God's presence in the darkness and knew it was real. A man who'd been pulled back from the brink for something. For a purpose. For a life that mattered, even when everything was falling apart.

Another battle had been won. Not because he was stronger or better, but because God had answered when he prayed. God had delivered him again. Not from the circumstances. The foreclosure notice was still real, the thirty-day deadline still looming. But the crushing weight, the suffocating darkness, the sense of being utterly helpless, that passed. Lifted. Retreated in the face of something stronger.

He sat back on his heels, breathing hard, his heart still racing but no longer from panic. From something else. From the aftermath of battle. From the realization that he'd just fought back with help he had won. He won because Jesus had finished it, finished the work on the cross!

He looked down at the envelope on the floor. It was still there, still pink, still screaming FORECLOSURE in red letters. But somehow, it didn't look as big anymore. Didn't feel as overwhelming. It was a problem, yes. A serious problem. But it wasn't the end of the world. It wasn't worth dying over.

He picked up the letter and read it again, this time with clearer eyes. Thirty days to respond. Options to explore. Possibility of loan modification. It wasn't a death sentence. It was a problem that needed solving.

He folded the letter carefully and set it on the kitchen counter. Then he gathered up the rest of the scattered mail, putting everything in a neat pile. His hands were steady now. His breathing was normal. The presence he'd felt was still there, quieter now but no less real. Like a hand on his shoulder. Like someone standing beside him.

He glanced at the clock. Three thirty. Jessie would be home around seven. She'd taken on extra work today, desperate for a few more dollars. A few hours to sit with this news, to process it, to figure out how to tell her.

The old John, the John from a week ago, would have spiraled back to the darkness during those four hours. Would have convinced himself that this was the final straw, that there was no way out, that he'd failed his family beyond redemption. But that John had died three nights ago. Or maybe not died, maybe been reborn. Transformed. Changed into someone who knew, really knew, that he wasn't alone.

He made himself a cup of coffee and sat at the kitchen table, the foreclosure notice in front of him. His thoughts drifted to the impossible task ahead: telling Jessie what had happened, admitting that his months of unemployment had led them to this point, confessing that he was responsible for putting their home, their security, even the children's stability at risk.

The shame was still there. The guilt was real. He had failed to provide for his family. He had let them down. Those were facts, and no amount of prayer would change them.

But beneath the shame and guilt was something else now. Something new. A certainty that even though he was responsible, even though he'd made mistakes, even though the situation was dire, he wasn't facing it alone.

Jessie would be devastated. She'd probably cry. She might even be angry, though she'd try to hide it. But he knew, with the same certainty he'd felt during his prayer, that she wouldn't give up. She wouldn't walk away. She wouldn't tell him he was worthless or that she'd be better off without him.

She would work with him to find a way. Even when there seemed to be no way. That was what faith looked like.

That's what she'd done in the backyard, after all. When there was no way, when death seemed inevitable, when the darkness had him surrounded, she'd found a way. God had shown her a way. And together, they'd fought back the darkness and won.

This was just another battle. Different circumstances, different challenges, but the same truth: they were in this together. Him, Jessie, and God. That's what Jessie had said in the backyard, and it was still true now.

You, me, and God. We're here together.

He took a sip of his coffee and stared at the pink envelope. Thirty days. They had thirty days to figure something out. Thirty days to explore options, to talk to the bank, to maybe find a lawyer who could help them navigate this. Thirty days wasn't a lot of time, but it was something. It was enough time to work out a plan, to come up with a solution. It was a chance to get it right, and that was so much better than the darkness of despair.

He carried something now that had been missing in his life. Jessie's support was everything, and Pastor Mike's guidance mattered, but beyond that, something deeper had returned, something that had been missing for months. He now had hope, real hope. It didn't waver when he thought about the empty bank account or the uncertain future. It came from knowing God was real, that God was present, that God had shown up in his darkest moment and saved him.

If God could do that, if God could send Jessie into the backyard at the exact moment he needed her, if God could meet him in his darkest hour, then maybe, just maybe, God could help them figure out this foreclosure thing too.

He didn't know how. He couldn't see the path forward. The numbers didn't add up, the timeline was impossibly short, and the obstacles seemed insurmountable. But he'd learned something in the past three days: God specialized in impossible situations. In making ways where there seemed to be no way. In bringing life out of death.

The backyard had taught him that.

So he sat at the kitchen table, drinking his coffee, waiting for his wife to come home. The foreclosure notice lay in front of him, still pink, still threatening. But it didn't own him anymore. It didn't define him. It didn't have the power to send him spiraling back into the dark place.

Because he'd been there. He'd been to the absolute bottom, to the place where death seemed like the only option. And he'd come back. God had pulled him back. Jessie had fought for him. And now he knew, really knew, that no matter how bad things got, no matter how impossible the situation seemed, he wasn't alone. The shadows had lost. Jesus was in charge now. Somehow, in some quiet, stubborn way, they were going to figure this out.

He took another sip of his coffee and waited for his wife to come home.

CHAPTER II

TOGETHER

Night settled over the kitchen. The darkness seemed to cling to the corners of the room. John sat alone at the table, papers fanned out in front of him like a losing hand of cards: foreclosure notice, bank statements, hastily written notes. He was staring at the numbers when he heard Jessie's car in the driveway. His heart began to race. He reminded himself that the kids were safe at his mother's house, she had agreed to take them to school in the morning, at least that was one thing he didn't have to worry about tonight.

He'd been sitting at the kitchen table for the past three hours, the pink foreclosure notice in front of him like an accusation, rehearsing what he would say in his head over and over. How he would explain the missed payments, the mounting bills, the quiet lies. How he would apologize for failing her, for failing their family, for letting things get this bad when it was his job to protect them, to keep this home safe and stable.

But now that she was actually here, now that he could hear her keys jingling as she set them on the entry table and her footsteps coming down the hall toward him, all his carefully prepared words evaporated, slipping away like mist before he could grasp them. His face felt hot, burning with shame that rose from his chest to his cheeks in a wave that made his vision blur at the edges.

He had already told her about the cryptocurrency scam. He had confessed that he had lost the five thousand dollars, most of their savings, to some faceless con artist on the internet. He had already had to see the look on her face when she realized just how foolish he had been, how desperate, how willing to believe in a miracle that was too good to be true.

That conversation had been one of the hardest of his life, but this, this would be worse.

Because the scam had been a mistake, a moment of stupid judgment born from desperation, but the foreclosure was the culmination of months of failure, months of not being able to provide, months of watching their bills pile up as he sent out resume after resume and got nothing back but silence or rejection.

This was all his fault. Every bit of it. And no amount of handyman work, no number of part-time jobs, no miracle employment opportunity was going to fix this mess. The math didn't work. The timeline was too short. They were going to lose the house, and it was because John Mitchell couldn't keep his family afloat.

He felt terrible watching her carry them both financially, doing everything she could to keep them going, while he could barely earn enough to pay even the light bill.

But even as the shame burned in his face and his stomach churned with dread, he felt something else, something new, something that had not been there three days ago or even three weeks ago. He was not alone anymore. He had help now, and hope. He was prepared to face this, not alone. He had tried that, and it had nearly killed him, but now he had Jessie, and he had something else, something he had experienced just hours ago on this very kitchen floor.

Prayer.

Real prayer. The kind where God actually showed up. The kind where you could feel His presence like electricity in the air. The kind that pushed back darkness and gave you strength you didn't have on your own.

He heard Jessie's footsteps getting closer. She was getting closer to the kitchen. In a few seconds, she'd walk through that doorway, and he'd have to tell her. Show her the pink envelope. Watch her face as she read the words "foreclosure proceedings" and "thirty days to respond."

But first, before any of that, they were going to pray.

Jessie appeared in the doorway, still in her work uniform, her hair pulled back, exhaustion written in every line of her face. She'd been working all day, pushing herself to the limit. Hours of carrying more than her share, all to keep their family afloat while he struggled to find work. And now he had to tell her it wasn't enough. That, despite all her sacrifices, all her extra hours, all her determination to hold things together, they were still going to lose the house.

Jessie stopped in the doorway. One look at John's face and she knew something was wrong. Fifteen years of marriage had made her fluent in the language of his silences and also the things not said. "What's wrong?" she asked, her voice already tight with concern.

He took a breath. His face was still burning, his hands trembling slightly. But his voice, when it came out, was steady.

"A lot," he said quietly. "But before we talk, I want to pray for guidance and strength."

Jessie stopped in her tracks, her breath catching in her throat. Her eyes widened, and for a long, stunned moment, she just stared at him like he'd spoken in a foreign language, as if every familiar word had been rearranged into something impossible to understand.

"Did you just say what I think you said?" she asked slowly, her eyes narrowing in disbelief as she tried to process his words.

He nodded. "I did. I want to pray with you, right here and now, before we talk about everything on this table," indicating the paperwork and bills spread out on the table.

He could see the surprise on her face. John Mitchell, who'd stopped praying months ago. John Mitchell, who'd refused to go to church, who'd pulled away from God, who'd let his faith wither into nothing. John Mitchell was asking to pray.

But beneath the shock, he saw something else. Hope. Fragile and tentative, like a candle flame in a dark room, trembling at the slightest movement yet stubbornly refusing to go out.

He nodded. "I did. I want to pray with you, right here and now, before we talk about everything on this table," he said, indicating the paperwork and bills spread out on the table. "Okay," she said softly, her voice barely above a whisper. She crossed the small, dimly lit kitchen and sat down in the chair next to him, reaching for his trembling hands. "Okay, let's pray," and he noticed something else too, her eyes never left his, never drifted to the paperwork on the table, and for that he loved her even more.

He took her hands in his, feeling how small they were, how rough from the hard work of the past few weeks. These hands had held him in the backyard, these hands had knocked a gun away and saved his life, these hands had refused to let him go, even when he had wanted nothing more than to disappear.

He bowed his head, and Jessie did the same.

For a moment, he didn't know what to say. The words felt like they would not come out, somehow tangled up with shame and fear and the weight of what he had to tell her, then he remembered what had happened earlier: the presence he'd felt, the warmth in his chest, the certainty that God was real and listening.

"Father," he began, his voice rough. "We need you. We need

Your guidance, Your help, Your direction. Everything has gone wrong, and we don't know what to do."

Beside him, she squeezed his hands tighter.

"We're scared," he continued, and he felt his voice breaking. "We're overwhelmed. We've made mistakes. I've made mistakes. And now we're facing consequences that feel too big to handle."

They prayed together, hands joined, the afternoon light slanting across the kitchen table. John continued praying.

"But we're here together," he said, his voice stronger. " And we know You're here too. We felt you in the backyard. I felt you today. And we're asking, we're begging, for your help. For your wisdom. For Your provision. For Your peace, even when everything feels like it is falling apart."

"Yes, Lord," she whispered, her own voice thick with emotion. "Please help us. Please show us what to do next."

"We don't know how this is going to work out," he said. "We don't know if we're going to lose everything. But we're choosing to trust You anyway. We're choosing to believe that You're with us, that You have a plan even when we can't see it."

The tears came, from both of them. But something else was happening too. Something he could feel building in the space between them, in the air around them, in the very atmosphere of the kitchen.

Hope. The kind that could exist alongside fear and tears and uncertainty. The kind that whispered, Even if the worst happens, you're going to be okay.

"Even if we have to find a new place to live," he prayed, the words coming from somewhere deep inside him," it's going to be okay. Because we have each other. And we have You. And that's enough. That has to be enough."

"Amen," she whispered. "Amen."

They sat there for a moment in silence, heads still bowed, hands still clasped. He could feel his heart beating, could hear her breathing, could sense something else: that same presence he'd felt earlier, that warmth, that certainty that they weren't alone.

And then Jessie went still, her eyes widening. "John," she said, her voice filled with wonder. "Do you feel that?"

They both sensed a change in the atmosphere, charged with something they could not name. The hairs on their arms lifting, not from cold but from the power of prayer moving through the room.

He opened his eyes and looked at her. Jessie was staring at her arms, her eyes wide with amazement. And then he looked down at his own arms and saw it, the same thing he'd seen earlier, the same thing that had made him stop and stare in wonder.

God's presence. Tangible, real, and undeniable.

He looked at Jessie, and she looked back at him, and in that moment, they both knew. This wasn't their imagination. This wasn't wishful thinking or emotional manipulation or the power of positive thinking.

This was real.

God was here. In their kitchen. With them. Confirming what he had experienced earlier, showing Jessie what he'd felt, making His presence known in a way that couldn't be explained away or rationalized.

He nodded slowly, unable to speak, tears still streaming down his face.

"He's here," she whispered, her voice trembling. "He's really here."

They sat there for several minutes, just feeling it, just being in it. The presence that pushed back fear and filled the empty spaces with something stronger than hope: with certainty. With peace. With the knowledge that no matter what happened, they weren't facing it alone.

Finally, he reached for the pink envelope on the table. His hands were steadier now, his breathing calmer. The shame was still there. He couldn't make that disappear. But it wasn't crushing him anymore. It wasn't defining him.

"There's something I need to show you," he said quietly.

He handed her the envelope, watching her face as she pulled out the letter. He saw her eyes scan the page, saw the moment when she registered what she was reading. Saw the color drain from her face as the words" foreclosure proceedings" and" thirty days" sank in.

"Oh, John," she whispered.

"I'm sorry," he said, his voice breaking again. "I'm so sorry. This is all my fault. I couldn't find work fast enough, couldn't keep up with the payments, couldn't provide for our family. And now we're going to lose the house, and it's because I failed you."

She set the letter down and looked at him. Her eyes were red from crying, her face was pale with shock, but there was something else there, too. Something that suprised him.

No anger. No blame. No accusation.

Just love. And determination. And that same certainty they'd both felt during the prayer.

"We're going to lose the house," she said slowly, as if testing the words, seeing how they felt. Then she said it again, stronger this time. "We're going to lose the house. And it's going to be okay."

He stared at her. "What?"

"It's going to be okay," she repeated, and now she was reaching for his hands again, holding them tight. "I don't know how. I don't know where we'll go or what we'll do. But John, did you feel what just happened? Did you feel His spirit here with us?"

He nodded, unable to speak.

"That's real," she said fiercely. "That presence, that peace, that certainty, that's real. And if God is with us, if He's really here with us, then we're going to be okay. Even if we have to find a new place to live. Even if we lose everything. We're going to be okay."

She was saying the same thing he had been thinking. The

same thing he'd prayed. The same truth that had settled in his heart during those hours of waiting for her to come home.

"I thought you'd be angry," he said quietly. "I thought you'd blame me."

"I'm not angry," she said, and he could hear the truth in her voice. " I'm scared. I'm overwhelmed. But I'm not angry. We're in this together, remember? You, me, and God. That's what I told you in the backyard, and it's still true now."

He felt something release deep in his heart, a crumbling and breaking down of the last wall he'd been holding up between himself and his wife. The wall that said he had to be strong, had to have all the answers, had to fix everything on his own.

"I don't know what to do," he admitted. "I don't know how to fix this."

"We'll figure it out," she said. "Together. We'll call the bank tomorrow and see what options we have. We'll talk to Pastor Mike, see if he knows of any resources we haven't though about. We'll look into loan modifications, payment plans, whatever we can find. And if none of that works, if we really do have to leave this house, then we'll find somewhere else. Somewhere smaller, somewhere cheaper. It won't be the end of the world."

"But the kids," he said. "Emma and Caleb. This is their home. Their rooms, their neighborhood, their school."

"They'll adjust," she said firmly. "Kids are resilient. And you know what they need more than this house? They need their dad. They need you alive and present and fighting. That's what matters. Not the address on our mailbox."

He looked at his wife, really looked at her, and saw the same woman who'd run into the backyard three nights ago with supernatural strength. The same woman who'd stood between him and death and declared that he would not give the enemy that victory.

She was doing it again. Standing between him and despair. Refusing to let the circumstances define them. Choosing hope even when there was no logical reason for it.

"For the first time in a long time," she said softly, "even though we have no reason to hope, hope feels good. Doesn't it?"

He nodded, feeling the truth of it settle in. "Yes. It does."

They sat there at the kitchen table, the foreclosure notice between them, their hands clasped together, the presence of God still tangible in the air around them. Outside, the sun was setting, painting the kitchen in shades of gold and amber. The light caught the tears on their faces, making them shine.

"We're going to be okay," she said again, like a promise, like a prayer, like a declaration of war against the darkness that wanted to consume them.

"We're going to be okay," he echoed, and for the first time since opening that pink envelope, he believed it.

Because something had changed them, because in that moment they had felt God's presence settle over them, steady and real, because they had prayed and He had answered, because they knew deeply, finally, that they weren't facing this alone.

The foreclosure was still real. The thirty-day deadline was still ticking. The problems were still massive and overwhelming and seemingly impossible to solve.

But they had something now that they did not have before. Something stronger than fear, more powerful than despair, more certain than the doubts and darkness they had both experienced over the past few weeks.

They had each other, they had God, and they had hope, and somehow miraculous grace found them and filled their hearts until they overflowed, a force both fierce and tender that shattered the darkness and flooded them with the light of grace.

CHAPTER 12

GRACE

Two weeks had slipped by in a blur. Two weeks of phone calls, tense meetings, and desperate attempts to find a solution that simply didn't exist. Two weeks of sitting with a lawyer friend, who had studied the numbers in grim silence before only shaking his head. Two weeks of facing bank representatives across polished desks, their expressions kind yet unyielding as they repeated, with practiced sympathy, that there was nothing more they could do.

They had spent those two weeks praying together every morning and every night, feeling God's presence, knowing He was with them, but still not seeing any way out.

The bank had made its position clear: they could drag this out for months, accumulating legal fees and damage to their credit, or they could sign a voluntary agreement to vacate, to quit-claim all the money they had paid into the house. The bank's attorney had been blunt but not unkind. If they cooperated, the bank would forgive the remaining debt and give them a clean break. If they fought it, they would lose anyway, but they would still leave with nothing and a financial black mark that would follow them for years. They had even tried to see if they could sell the house and at least come out with enough money to start over, but the housing market was just upside down; there was really no choice left.

So they had made the hardest decision of their lives: they had signed the papers agreeing to leave voluntarily within thirty days. The bank still required a formal legal notice as a legal formality, something about protecting its interests and documenting the process, even though John and Jessie had already agreed to go.

In the first two weeks, they had tried everything to find a solution. The next two weeks, they had searched for rental properties they could afford on Jessie's income and his sporadic handyman work, all the while packing boxes, explaining to Emma and Caleb that they were going to have to move, and watching their children's faces turn sad with questions, confusion, and fear, holding onto hope even when every practical indicator said there was no hope to be had.

And now, those thirty days had passed. Time was up. It was eleven o'clock on a Tuesday morning. The kids were at school, unaware that today was the day the deputy sheriff would deliver the final notice, the legal formality the bank insisted on even though they had already agreed to leave. The paperwork would give them three days, but they had already packed most of their belongings. They had made peace with the idea that this was one fight they had lost.

The house was full of boxes, their entire life carefully packed up and ready to be moved to somewhere new, somewhere unfamiliar. They still hadn't found a place that felt right or even truly livable, despite weeks of searching and endless online listings. But they'd run out of time to look.

John and Jessie sat at the kitchen table, the same worn table where they'd prayed together weeks ago, where they'd felt God's presence so tangibly and overwhelmingly that the hairs on their arms had stood up and their eyes had filled with tears. The same table where they'd decided to trust God even if they lost everything, even if their plans fell apart and their future looked nothing like what they had imagined.

Now, they were about to find out what "everything" really meant in all its complicated, unsettling detail.

He reached across the table and took her hand. She squeezed back, her grip tight, her eyes red from crying. They had both done a lot of crying over the past few weeks, but they had also done a lot of praying, and somehow, impossibly, they had maintained that sense of peace, that certainty that even though they were losing their home, they were still going to be okay.

"You, me, and God," she whispered, echoing the words she had spoken in the backyard. "We're in this together."

"Together," he agreed.

Then they heard it.

A sharp, authoritative rapping at the front door. This was not the friendly knock of a neighbor or the tentative tap of a delivery person. This was the kind of knock that demanded attention, that announced official business, that quickened your pulse even before you opened the door.

The kind of knock that only came from law enforcement.

John and Jessie looked at each other. This was it. The sheriff's deputy is here to serve the final legal notice. Here to tell them they had seventy-two hours to vacate the property. Here to make it official that they were losing their home.

He stood up slowly, his legs feeling weak. Jessie stood with him, her hand still gripping his. Together, they walked to the front door.

He opened it, and Jessie's grip tightened on his hand.

Standing on their front porch, in full uniform with a clipboard in his hand, was Sheriff's Deputy Gerald Morrison. The same Gerald Morrison who'd been in John's graduating class at the high school. Gerald, who'd played on the same football team. Gerald, who'd been at their wedding fifteen years ago.

Gerald's face was bright red, his expression a mixture of professional duty and personal anguish.

"John," Gerald said, his voice strained. "Jessie. I'm so sorry. Truly, I am."

He held out a piece of paper, his hand shaking slightly. "I have to serve you with this legal notice. You have three days to vacate the property. I'm so, so sorry."

John took the paper, but he couldn't seem to focus on the words. Three days. Seventy-two hours. And then they'd be out on the street with all their belongings and nowhere to go.

"It's okay, Gerald," he heard himself say, though his voice sounded distant, hollow. "You're just doing your job."

Gerald looked like he might cry. "If there was anything I could do—"

"We know," Jessie said gently. "We know."

John was staring at the paper in his hand, at the official seal, the legal language, and the deadline that felt like a death sentence. He knew they would not be homeless, not really; they could stay with family, or maybe her parents would take them in for a while. People did it all the time.

But the knowing did not ease anything. The weight was still there, pressing down on both of them. They would have shelter, yes, and food, and that was more than so many others had. He understood that, and he was grateful for it, even now. But this house, their house, the place where his daughter had taken her first steps, where they had marked each birthday on the doorframe in the hallway, where every room held the small, sacred accumulation of their lives together, that would be gone forever.

The loss felt both enormous and trivial at once, and he didn't know which feeling to trust.

He read the deadline again, as if the numbers might rearrange themselves into something more forgiving. They didn't. The paper trembled in his grip. Everything felt unsteady.

And then, movement. Just at the edge of his vision. Something made him lift his head, made him turn toward the street without knowing why.

He looked up, past Gerald, past the legal notice, to the street beyond.

A large commercial van was pulling up to the curb. Not a moving van. This was something else. Something sleek and professional, with a logo emblazoned on the side in elegant script.

H Media Group.

A cold wave of dread hit him. Were they reporters? His mind raced through worst-case scenarios. TV cameras capturing the family that couldn't make it. The neighbors watching from behind their curtains as his failure was documented for the evening news. His face broadcast to thousands of strangers, forever attached to this moment, this loss.

He briefly imagined a slickly dressed woman with perfect hair and makeup shoving a microphone in their faces, asking the question, How does this make you feel? Of course, hoping that tears would be part of the reply, the TV reporter's best friend, a distraught human tragedy, complete with crying and tears.

A man got out of the van. John exhaled slightly. No camera crew, no microphone, but his brief relief gave way to confusion as he noticed that this was a man in an expensive suit carrying a leather briefcase, walking with the confident stride of someone who knew exactly what he was doing and had the authority to do it.

The man walked up the driveway, nodding politely to Gerald, and extended his hand to John.

"Mr. Mitchell? My name is Simon Atwater, from Atwater, Bine, and Brice. I'm an attorney, and I have filed papers to stop this foreclosure."

He stared at him. The words made sense individually, but strung together like that, they did not compute. An attorney? Filing papers? Stopping the foreclosure? "But I can't afford an attorney," he said, and even as the words left his mouth, he heard how odd they sounded.

It struck him as strange to be saying it out loud, not really knowing what was actually happening.

Simon Atwater smiled. "It is covered, Mr. Mitchell, all of it. Now, can we step inside? I will fill you in on all the details."

He turned to Gerald and handed him a piece of paper. John caught a glimpse of official-looking letterhead and what he thought might be the word "injunction," but his mind could not grasp it. His brain was moving too slowly as letters swam before his eyes, and he was not sure what he was seeing.

Gerald looked at the paper, his eyes widening. "This is legitimate?"

"Completely," Simon said. "The foreclosure proceedings have been stayed pending resolution of the matter, and you can verify with the court if you would like."

Gerald looked at him, his expression transforming from anguish to bewilderment. "John, I do not know what is going on, but this appears to be valid. The notice has been cancelled. You don't have to leave."

Then Gerald began walking back to his patrol car, shaking his head in amazement, and Simon Atwater was standing on John's front porch with a briefcase full of legal documents and a smile that suggested he knew something John did not.

"Can we sit down?" Simon asked. "This might take a few minutes to explain."

John and Jessie led him to the kitchen table in a daze. They sat down, and Simon opened his briefcase and pulled out a stack of papers.

"First," Simon said, "let me tell you a bit about who I work for. The Henderson Media Group is a conglomerate that owns several large companies: television stations, news-papers, and digital media platforms. The owner, Mr. Augustus Henderson, is a very successful businessman, and more importantly for your situation, he is a very generous man."

Henderson. The name stirred something, a dim memory he couldn't quite grasp, but he was still feeling confused about what was happening.

"Mr. Henderson will be here shortly," Simon continued. "He wanted to speak with you personally, but in the meantime, I can tell you that he has taken steps to resolve your financial situation. The details are in these documents, but the short version is."

"Wait," John interrupted, his brain finally starting to catch up. "I do not understand. Why would this Mr. Henderson care about our foreclosure? I do not even know him."

Simon smiled. "Mr. Henderson will be arriving any moment, and I think it is better if he explains it himself."

He opened his mouth to ask another question, but before he could speak, there was a knock at the door. A friendly, almost casual tapping.

Jessie went to answer it. John saw her freeze in the doorway, her hand flying to her mouth. He heard a man's voice say, "Had any good ice cream lately?"

A moment later, she was leading an older man into the kitchen. He was probably in his seventies, with silver hair and kind eyes, dressed in casual but expensive clothes. He walked with the easy confidence of someone who'd been successful for so long that he no longer needed to prove anything to anyone.

And he was smiling at John like they were old friends.

"Mr. Mitchell," the man said warmly, extending his hand. "It's good to finally meet you properly."

He stood up automatically, shaking the man's hand, his mind racing. Finally meet him properly? What did that mean? He'd never seen this man before in his life.

"I don't understand," he said.

The older man's smile widened. "Let me ask you a question, Mr. Mitchell. You did a plumbing job for an elderly woman recently, didn't you? A water heater replacement, some water line work, a kitchen faucet?"

His mouth went dry. "Yes," he said slowly. "Yes, I did. Mrs. Henderson. She was very kind."

And then it hit him. Henderson. Mrs. Henderson. Henderson Media Group.

The recognition must have shown on his face because the older man nodded. "Yes," he said gently. "That was my mother."

He felt like the floor had slipped out from under him. Mrs. Henderson, the sweet elderly woman who'd paid him $125 for six hours of work, who'd brought him lemonade and cookies, who'd told him he was a good man, was this man's mother?

"You see, John," Mr. Henderson continued, gesturing for everyone to sit back down," I own several very large companies. I've been blessed with considerable success in my business ventures. And I've taken steps to fix this problem you're having."

John's heart was pounding. "But we owe more than three hundred thousand dollars. The mortgage, the back payments, the fees. It's too much. There's no way to—"

His voice trailed off as Mr. Henderson held up a hand.

"John," Mr. Henderson said, his voice kind but firm, "the Henderson Group has paid off your outstanding balance on your home, all of it. You will not be moving today or any day, this is your house, free and clear. There are no requirements to meet, no strings to worry about."

Silence.

Complete, absolute silence that seemed to stretch and echo through the kitchen.

He stared at Mr. Henderson. His mouth was open, but no words would come out. His brain had simply stopped processing. Paid off? Three hundred thousand dollars? Free and clear?

"I... but... I don't... how can you..." He stammered, then fell silent again.

Mr. Henderson leaned forward, his expression serious now.

"My mother is the most important person in my world, John. But sometimes I get too busy. Sometimes I let my work consume me, and I don't pay enough attention to the people who matter most. Last month, my mother's water heater broke. I was caught up in a major business deal and didn't even realize it until later. I should have noticed something was wrong, but I was too distracted by work. I wasn't there for her when she needed me."

He paused, his eyes meeting John's. "And then you showed up. You came into her home, and you fixed her problem. You were kind to her. You treated her with respect and dignity. You charged her a fraction of what you could have, even though you were desperate for money yourself. You helped my mother at a time when she needed it most, at a time when I couldn't be there."

John felt tears burning in his eyes. "I just... it was just a plumbing job. It wasn't anything special."

"It was special to her," Mr. Henderson said firmly. "And it is special to me. Last year, my company made a lot of money, John, more money than I know what to do with, honestly, and believe it or not, the price of paying off your home is not as big a deal as you think. I have been so blessed in my business that this small amount represents less than a week of revenue.

He held up his hand again as John started to speak. "And before you say anything, let me just say this: you were kind to my mother. You treated her like she mattered." He paused, his voice softening. "You see, John, my mother is like so many of her generation. She doesn't want to feel dependent on others to pay her bills. Even me. So when you allowed her to pay for those repairs herself, you gave her something no one else could have given her at that moment.

You gave her pride in her ability to handle a difficult situation all by herself, without having to rely on me to arrange it and pay for it. I only found out about it after you'd already repaired it, and for a price she could afford to pay." His eyes held John's. "That, my friend, is something so profound you cannot put a price on it.

That kindness, that generosity, that character, what you gave my mother, it means more to me than any amount of money."

He just stared at him, his mouth still open, no words coming out. This couldn't be real. This couldn't be happening. People didn't just pay off other people's mortgages. Miracles like this didn't happen in real life.

But Mr. Henderson was still talking, still smiling, still looking at John like erasing someone's debt was the most natural thing in the world.

"I think the word you're looking for," Mr. Henderson said gently, is "thank you."

"Yes," he managed to choke out. " Yes, of course. Thank you. Thank you, Mr. Henderson. I don't... I can't..."

"Call me Gus," Mr. Henderson said, standing up and extending his hand again. "All my friends call me Gus. And I have a feeling we're going to be friends, John."

John stood up on shaky legs and shook Gus Henderson's hand. The older man's grip was firm, warm, and real. This was really happening. This was real.

Mr. Henderson stood up. As they shook hands, he paused and met John's eyes. "John, I have a confession to make. I have not always been close to God, but recently I was reminded that God does amazing things in ways we cannot always figure out."

He took a breath. "I was in town a few weeks ago to take care of some paperwork, and I stopped by an ice cream shop because I had some time between meetings. Something amazing happened there. A group of people were praying openly, in public, and I felt something I hadn't felt in years: the presence of faith and hope."

His voice grew quieter. "I had no idea what would happen in the future, but in that moment, I learned a little about human compassion and faith. This was a group of people praying for a man who was in trouble. Believers gathered together to pray for a family that was hurting, this family needed help. I was touched beyond measure, and I prayed for the first time in a long time."

He shook his head slightly, a smile forming. "Then later, when my mother had that emergency with her water heater, and I found out that you were the man they were praying for and your wife was part of those people praying..." He paused. "I just knew that this entire situation was really God working all along in ways that, frankly, are just amazing. "You know, at my age, I should not be surprised when God moves in amazing ways, but that is how He steps into our lives; even when we might not see it, He always has a plan."

Mr. Henderson stepped back, nodding to the attorney.

Simon Atwater rose from his chair, gathering the papers into a neat stack. "Before we can finalize everything," he said, "I'll need you both to call my office and set up a time to come in and sign the release forms. Once those are signed, the deed can be formally satisfied and transferred into your names, free and clear."

John nodded, emotion catching in his throat. "Thank you... both of you," he said quietly. "For this... For this miracle."

He handed John a folder thick with legal documents, then followed Gus Henderson toward the door.

At the threshold, Gus turned back. "Oh, and John? My mother told me you're good with your hands. If you're looking for work, I could use someone to help maintain some of my properties. Nothing fancy, just general handyman work. But it would be steady, and it pays well. Think about it."

And then they were gone, walking back to the van with the H Media Group logo, leaving John and Jessie standing in their kitchen, surrounded by boxes they no longer needed to move, holding a folder full of documents that said their house was going to be paid off.

For a long moment, neither of them moved. Neither of them spoke. They just stood there, staring at each other, trying to process everything.

Finally, Jessie broke the silence.

"John," she whispered, her voice shaking. "What just happened?"

He looked down at the folder in his hands. Then he looked at his wife, at the boxes stacked around them, at the kitchen table where they'd prayed together days ago, and felt God's presence so tangibly.

And suddenly, he understood.

"God just happened," he said, his voice filled with wonder. "That's what grace is all about."

Grace. The weight of grace. Heavy because it cost Jesus everything. Heavy because it asked me to lay down my pride, my self-sufficiency, my illusion of control. Heavy because it confronted the truth I didn't want to face: that I could not save myself, could not repair what I had broken, could not climb out of the pit on my own.

But also light, a steady, shining light. Light because it carried me when I could not stand, light because it came as a gift I could never earn, light because it broke through my darkness and whispered what every soul longs to hear: you are loved, you are valued, you are worth saving. I have felt that light before, and today I have seen grace move in ways I never imagined was possible.

I see now that grace was never absent; I just didn't understood it until now. This impossible gift we never deserved, never earned, never could have imagined. Grace that delivered us from the pit. Grace that brought us back into life, into light, into all the beauty we thought we'd lost forever. It's overwhelming. It's humbling. It's heavier than any burden and lighter than air.

The weight of grace.

He set the folder down on the kitchen table and pulled her into his arms. She was crying now, great sobs of relief and joy and disbelief. He was crying too, tears streaming down his face, his body shaking with the force of emotions they couldn't name.

They stood there in the kitchen, their kitchen, in the house that was now paid off and truly theirs, and they held each other and cried and laughed, trying to comprehend the incomprehensible.

God had shown up again, not in the way they had expected, not in the way they had prayed for, but in a way that was so perfectly, impossibly, miraculously God that there was no other explanation.

They had been ready to lose everything. They had packed their boxes, said goodbye to their home, and prepared to start over with nothing. They had chosen to trust God even when every circumstance said there was no reason to hope.

And God had answered, not by gradually changing their circumstances, not by giving them just enough to scrape by, but by completely, overwhelmingly, abundantly providing for them in a way they never could have dreamed He would.

"We're not moving," she said, her voice muffled against his shoulder. "We're not moving. We get to stay."

"We get to stay," he echoed, the words feeling surreal even as he said them.

They pulled apart, looking at each other with tear-streaked faces and wondering eyes. And then, without discussing it, without planning it, they both knew what they needed to do.

They knelt right there in the kitchen, in the same spot where he had fallen to his knees weeks ago when the foreclosure notice had arrived. The same spot where he'd felt that crushing weight of despair and then experienced God's presence pushing back the darkness.

And they prayed.

The prayers rising now were prayers of thanksgiving, of gratitude, of worship. Prayers filled with wonder at a God who showed up in backyards and kitchens, in impossible situations. He said, "I've got you. You're mine. You were never alone."

"Thank You," he prayed, his voice thick with emotion. "Thank you for saving my life. Thank you for sending Jessie. Thank you for not giving up on me when I gave up on myself. Thank You for this house, for this miracle, for showing us that You're real and You're here and You care about every detail of our lives."

"Thank you," Jessie added, her hand gripping his. "Thank You for grace. For showing us what it really means. For loving us even when we don't deserve it. For providing for us in ways we never could have imagined."

They stayed there for a long time, kneeling on the kitchen floor, praying and crying and feeling that same presence they'd felt before. That warmth, that certainty, that undeniable reality of God with them.

Eventually, they stood up. The boxes were still there, packed and ready to move. But now they could unpack them. Now they could put everything back where it belonged. Now they could stay.

John looked at Jessie, and she looked back at him, and they both started laughing. The sound bubbled up from somewhere deep, joyful and incredulous, the laughter of people who'd just witnessed a miracle.

"We need to call the kids," she said. "They need to know we are not moving."

"We need to call Pastor Mike," he added. "He's not going to believe this."

"We need to call everyone," Jessie said, pulling out her phone. "We need to tell everyone what God just did."

But first, they just stood there in their kitchen, in their house, holding each other and marveling at the weight of grace. At how heavy it was: the cost, the surrender, the humility required to receive it. And at how light it was: the freedom, the joy, the overwhelming relief of being held up by something stronger than yourself.

He thought about the backyard, about the gun in his hand, about how close he'd come to ending everything. And he thought about Mrs. Henderson, about charging her less for a job that should have cost much more, about being kind simply because it was the right thing to do.

He knew that this miracle was not a normal occurrence. Just because you trusted God did not mean that someone would appear and provide a miracle; they had been prepared to leave, they had been prepared to start over again, and they were amazed by what had happened and in the way it happened that was the real miracle.

They had no idea that God was weaving together a story of redemption more profound than anything they could have imagined. That's what grace did. It showed up in unexpected ways. It multiplied small acts of kindness into overwhelming provision. It took broken people and broken situations and somehow, impossibly, made them whole.

The weight of grace. Heavy and light at the same time. Costly and free. Earned and unearned. Deserved and undeserved. It was grace that had saved his life in the backyard. Grace that had held him up when he couldn't stand on his own.

The same grace that had brought him and Jessie together in prayer and shown them God's presence was real. And now, grace they never could have imagined had paid off their house and given them a future they thought they'd lost

He looked around the kitchen one more time: at the boxes they wouldn't need to move, at the table where they'd prayed, at the spot where he'd fallen to his knees only days ago and experienced God's presence.

This was their home. Not because they'd earned it or deserved it or managed to save it through their own efforts. But because grace had shown up and said, *This is yours. Not because of what you've done, but because of who I am.*

That was the weight of grace.

And it was beautiful.

AUTHORS NOTE

AUTHOR'S NOTE

If you or someone you know is struggling with thoughts of suicide, please reach out for help. You are not alone. You are loved. And you are worth saving.

National Suicide Prevention Lifeline: 988

Crisis Text Line: Text HOME to 741741

Website: suicidepreventionlifeline.org

This story deals with themes of depression, financial hardship, and faith crisis. While these are difficult topics, they are also real experiences that many people face. If John's story resonates with you, please know that help is available and hope is real.

Grace is real. You are valued. You are loved.

ABOUT THE AUTHOR

Timothy K. Franklin is an author who writes about faith, family, and biblical living, not from a place of perfection but from the honest recognition that none of us are perfect. This is precisely why we need God, Jesus, and the Holy Spirit.

Drawing from real-life stories and Scripture, Timothy explores how Christian faith shapes daily decisions. From marriage and parenting to work and community, he writes with transparency about the human condition and its struggles and shortcomings. He believes that authentic faith is not about having it all figured out, but about surrendering to Christ and allowing His Spirit to transform us.

His writing is grounded in the conviction that God's Word speaks directly to how we live, offering practical wisdom for those seeking to honor God in their everyday lives. Timothy believes that true meaning comes not from abstract ideals or personal achievement, but from obedience to Christ and His design for the human condition, and from the grace that sustains us when we fall short.

BONUS CONTENT

A Gift for Readers
The Official Soundtrack of
The Weight of Grace
A collection of 11 original songs
created to accompany the journey.
StrongHopeMusic.com
Answer 3 brief questions to access your download

REQUEST

ENJOYED THIS BOOK?

If The Weight of Grace encouraged your faith or spoke to your heart, I invite you to share your thoughts with other readers by leaving a review on Barnes & Noble, Amazon, Walmart, Target, and Books-A-Million, or wherever you purchased this book.

Your feedback helps others discover stories that point toward God's truth and hope.

To stay connected and hear about upcoming releases, including *The Fire of Faith* and *The Eternal Truth*, visit StrongHope-Media.com. I would be honored to share more of this journey with you.

Thank you for reading.

Timothy K. Franklin